"I Didn't Realize That I Was Capable of Tenderness,"

he said. "This morning I let go with you. I trusted you."

Her face was bright red, but she didn't look away. "I...trusted you, too." Her expression said more than she wanted it to, and she knew that he could read the worshipful look in her eyes.

His breath caught at that look, and he let go of her hand. "Don't ever try to build a wall around me," he said unexpectedly, staring at her. "I'll stay with you as long as the doors remain open."

"I knew that the first time I saw you," she said quietly. "No ties. No strings. I won't try to possess you."

He wondered what she would do when she knew the truth about him....

Dear Reader,

Welcome to Silhouette! Our goal is to give you hours of unbeatable reading pleasure, and we hope you'll enjoy each month's six new Silhouette Desires. These sensual, provocative love stories are both believable and compelling—sometimes they're poignant, sometimes humorous, but always enjoyable.

Indulge yourself. Experience all the passion and excitement of falling in love along with our heroine as she meets the irresistible man of her dreams and together they overcome all obstacles in the path to a happy ending.

If this is your first Desire, I hope it'll be the first of many. If you're already a Silhouette Desire reader, thanks for your support! Look for some of your favorite authors in the coming months: Stephanie James, Diana Palmer, Dixie Browning, Ann Major and Doreen Owens Malek, to name just a few.

Happy reading!

Isabel Swift
Senior Editor

SDRL-7/85

DIANA PALMER
The Tender Stranger

Silhouette Desire

Published by Silhouette Books New York

America's Publisher of Contemporary Romance

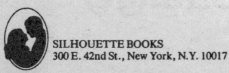

SILHOUETTE BOOKS
300 E. 42nd St., New York, N.Y. 10017

Copyright © 1985 by Diana Palmer

Distributed by Pocket Books

ISBN: 0-373-05230-8

First Silhouette Books printing September 1985

10 9 8 7 6 5 4 3 2 1

America's Publisher of Contemporary Romance

Printed in the U.S.A.

DIANA PALMER

is a prolific romance writer who got her start as a newspaper reporter. Accustomed to the daily deadlines of a journalist, she has no problem with writer's block. In fact, she averages a book every two months. Diana, now the mother of a young son, met and married her husband within one week: "It was just like something from one of my books."

To Patricia and Bob Major, my aunt and uncle,
who introduced me to the delights of
San Francisco, Napa Valley and Stinson Beach

One

The seat was much too low for his tall frame; he had barely enough room without the paraphernalia his companion was shifting in her own seat. He gave her a short glare through deep brown eyes. She flushed, her gaze dropping to her lap as she tucked her huge purse on the other side of her and struggled with her seat belt.

He sighed, watching her. A spinster, he thought unkindly. From her flyaway brown hair to the eyes under those wire-rimmed glasses, from her bulky white sweater down to her long gray skirt and sensible gray shoes, she was definitely someone's unclaimed treasure. He turned his eyes back to the too-narrow aisle. Damn budget airlines, he thought furiously. If he hadn't missed the flight he'd booked, he wouldn't be trying to fit into this sardine can of a seat. Next to Miss Frump here.

He didn't like women. Never less than now, when he was forced to endure this particular woman's company for several hundred miles from San Antonio down to Veracruz, Mexico. He glanced sideways again irritably. She was shifting books now. Books, for God's sake! Didn't she know what the baggage hold was for?

"You should have reserved a seat for them," he muttered, glaring at a stack of what was obviously romance novels.

She swallowed, a little intimidated as her eyes swept over a muscular physique, blond hair and a face that looked positively hostile. He had nice hands, though. Very lean and tanned and strong-looking. Scars on the back of one of them...

"I'm sorry," she murmured, avoiding his eyes. "I've just come from a romance writer's auto-graphing in San Antonio. These—these are auto-graphed copies I'm taking back for friends after my Mexican holiday, and I was afraid to trust them to the luggage compartment."

"Priceless gems?" he asked humorlessly, giving them a speaking glare as she tucked the sack-ful under her seat.

"To some people, yes," she acknowledged. Her face tautened and she didn't look at him again. She cast nervous glances out the window while the air-plane began to hum and the flight crew began once more the tedious demonstration of the safety equipment. He sighed impatiently and folded his arms across his broad chest, over the rumpled khaki shirt he wore. He leaned his head back, staring blankly at the stewardess. She was a beauty, but he wasn't interested. He hadn't been interested in women for quite a few years, except to satisfy an infrequent need. He laughed shortly, glancing at the prim little woman next to him. He wondered if she knew anything about those infrequent needs, and decided that she didn't. She looked as chaste as a nun, with her nervous eyes and hands. She had nice hands, though, he thought, pursing his lips as he studied them. Long fingers, very graceful, and no polish. They were the hands of a lady.

It irritated him that he'd noticed that. He glared harder at her.

That caught her attention. It was one thing to be impatiently tolerated, but she didn't like that superior glare. She turned and glared back at him. Something danced briefly in his dark eyes before he turned them back to the stewardess.

So she had fire, he thought. That was unexpected in a prim little nun. He wondered if she was a librarian. Yes, that would explain her fascination with books. And love stories...probably she was starving for a little love of her own. His eyes darkened. Stupid men, he thought, to overlook a feisty little thing like that just because of the glitter and paint that drew them to her more liberated counterparts.

There was murmuring coming from beside him. His sensitive ears caught a few feverish words: "Hail Mary, full of grace..."

It couldn't be! He turned, his eyes wide and stunned. Was she a nun?

She caught him looking at her and bit her lip self-consciously. "Habit," she breathed. "My best friend was Catholic. She taught me the rosary and we always recited it together when we flew. Personally," she whispered, wide-eyed, "I don't think there's anyone up there in the cockpit flying this thing!"

His eyebrows levered up. "You don't?"

She leaned toward him. "Do you ever see anybody in there?" She nodded toward the cockpit. "The door's always closed. If there isn't anything to hide, why do they close the door?"

He began to smile reluctantly. "Perhaps they're concealing a robot pilot?"

"More likely, they've got the pilot roped into his seat and they don't want us knowing it." She laughed softly, and it changed her face. With the right cosmetics and a haircut that didn't leave her soft hair unruly and half wild, she might not be bad-looking.

"You've been reading too many of those," he observed, gesturing toward the sack of books.

"Guilty." She sighed. "I suppose we need dreams sometimes. They keep reality at bay."

"Reality is better," he replied. "It has no illusions to spoil."

"I'd rather have my illusions."

He studied her openly. Wide, bow-shaped mouth, straight nose, wide-spaced pale gray eyes, heart-shaped face. She had a stubborn chin, too, and he smiled slowly. "You're a strange little creature," he said.

"I'm not little," she returned. "I'm five feet six."

He shrugged. "I'm over six feet. To me, you're little."

"I won't argue that," she said with a shy smile.

He chuckled. "Do you have a name?"

"Danielle. Danielle St. Clair. I own a bookstore in Greenville, South Carolina."

Yes, that fit her image to a T. "I'm called Dutch," he returned. "But my name is Eric van Meer."

"Are you Dutch?" she asked.

He nodded. "My parents were."

"It must be nice, having parents," she said with unconscious wistfulness. "I was small when I lost both of mine. I don't even have a cousin."

His eyes darkened and he turned his face away. "I hope they serve lunch on this flight," he remarked, changing the subject with brutal abruptness. "I haven't had anything since last night."

"You must be starved!" she exclaimed. She began to dig in her bag as the plane jerked and eased toward the runway. "I have a piece of cake left over from the autograph party. I didn't have time to eat it. Would you like it?'' she asked, and offered him a slice of coconut cake.

He smiled slowly. ''No. I'll wait. But thank you.''

She shrugged. ''I don't really need it. I'm trying to lose about twenty pounds.''

His eyes went over her. She was a little overweight. Not fat, just nicely rounded. He almost told her so. But then he remembered what treacherous creatures women were, and bit back the hasty words. He had concerns of his own, and no time for little spinsters. He leaned back and closed his eyes, shutting her out.

The flight passed uneventfully, but if he'd hoped to walk off the plane in Veracruz and forget about his seatmate, he was doomed to disappointment. When the plane finally rolled to a stop she stepped out into the aisle, juggling her luggage, and the sack containing her books broke into a thousand pieces.

Dutch tried not to laugh at the horrified expression on her face as he gathered the books quickly together and threw them into her seat, then herded her out of the aisle.

''Oh, Lord,'' she moaned, looking as if fate and the almighty were out to get her.

''Most travelers carry a spare bag inside their suitcases,'' he said hopefully as the other passengers filed out.

She looked up at him helplessly, all big gray eyes and shy pleading, and for an instant he actually forgot what he was saying. Her complexion was exquisite, he thought. He would have bet that she hardly ever used, or needed to use, beauty creams.

"Spare bag?" she echoed. "Spare bag!" She grinned. "Yes, of course." She shifted restlessly.

"Well?" he prompted gently.

She pointed to the overhead rack.

"We'll wait for everyone else to get off," he said. "Mine's up there, too; it's all right. No big deal."

She brushed back strands of wild hair and looked hunted. "I'm so organized back home," she muttered. "Not a stick of furniture out of place. But let me get outside the city limits of Greenville and I can't stick a fork on a plate without help."

He couldn't help laughing. "We'll get you sorted out," he said. "Where are you booked?"

"Book...oh, the hotel? It's the Mirador," she said.

Fate, he thought with a wistful smile. "That's where my reservation is," he said.

Her face lit up, and the look in her eyes faintly embarrassed him. She was gazing at him with a mixture of blind trust and hopeful expectation.

"Do you know the hotel? I mean, have you been here before?" she faltered, trying not to pry.

"Several times," he confessed. "I come down here once or twice a year when I need to get away." He glanced around. "Let's go."

He got down her suitcase and helped her extricate the spare bag from the case with a wry glance at the neat cotton nightgowns and underwear. She blushed wildly at that careless scrutiny, and he turned his attention to her books, packing them neatly and deftly.

She followed him out of the plane with gratitude shining on her face. She could have kissed him for not making fun of her, for helping her out. Imagine, she thought, a man like that actually doing something for her!

"I'm sorry to have been so much trouble," she blurted out, almost running to keep up with him as they headed toward customs and immigration. She was searching desperately for her passport, and missed the indulgent smile that softened his hard features momentarily.

"No trouble at all," he replied. "Got your passport?"

She sighed, holding it up. "Thank God I did something right," she moaned. "I've never even used it before."

"First time out of the States?" he asked pleasantly as they waited in line.

"First time out in Greenville, actually," she confessed. "I just turned twenty-six. I thought I'd better do something adventurous fast, before I ran out of time."

He frowned. "My God, twenty-six isn't old," he said.

"No," she agreed. "But it isn't terribly young, either." She didn't look at him. Her eyes were quiet and sad, and she was thinking back of all the long years of loneliness.

"Is there a man?" he asked without quite knowing why.

She laughed with a cynicism that actually surprised him, and the wide eyes that looked up into his seemed ancient. "I have no illusions at all about myself," she said, and moved ahead with her huge purse.

He stared at her straight back with mingled emotions, confusing emotions. Why should it matter to him that she was alone? He shook his head and glanced around him to break the spell. It was none of his business.

Minutes later she was through customs. She almost waited for her tall companion, but she thought that one way or another, she'd caused him enough trouble. The tour company had provided transfers from the airport to the hotel, but a cab seemed much more inviting and less crowded. She managed to hail one, and with her bag of books and suitcase, bustled herself into it.

"Hotel Mirador," she said.

The cab driver smiled broadly and gunned the engine as he pulled out into the crowded street. Dani, full of new experiences and delightful sensations, tried to look everywhere at once. The Bay of Campeche was blue and delightful, and there were glimpses of palms and sand and many hotels. Veracruz was founded in the early 1500s and looked as many old cities of that period did, its architecture alternating between the days of piracy and the space age. Dani would have loved to dive straight into some sight-seeing, but she was already uncomfortable in the formidable heat, and she knew it would be foolish to rush out without letting her body acclimate itself to its new environment.

As she gazed at the rows of hotels, the driver pulled into one of them, a two-story white building with graceful arches and a profusion of blooming flowers. It had only been a few minutes' ride from the airport, but the fare was confusing. And a little intimidating. Twenty dollars, just for several miles. But perhaps it was the custom, she thought, and paid him uncomplainingly.

He grinned broadly again, tipped his hat, and left her at the reservation desk.

She gave the clerk her name and waited with bated breath until her reservation was found. Finally, she had a room. Everything would be all right.

The room was nice. It overlooked the city, unfortunately, not the beautiful bay. But she hadn't expected much for the wonderfully low rates that had come with the package tour. She took off her sweater, amazed that it had felt so comfortable back in the States where it was early spring. It was much too heavy here, where the temperature was blazing hot even with the air-conditioning turned up. She stared out the window at the city. Mexico. It was like a dream come true. She'd scrimped and saved for two years to afford this trip. Even so, she'd had to come during the off-season, which was her busiest time back home. She'd left her friend Harriett Gaynor watching the bookstore in her absence. Go, Harriett had coaxed. Live a little.

She looked at herself in the mirror and grimaced. Live a little, ha! What a pity she hadn't looked like that gorgeous stewardess on the plane. Perhaps then the blond giant would have given her a second glance, or something besides the reluctant pity she'd read in his dark eyes.

She turned away from her reflection and began to unpack her suitcase. There was no use kidding herself that he'd helped her for any reason other than expediency. He could hardly walk right over her precious books. With a sigh she drew out her blouses and hung them up.

Two

By late afternoon Dani felt up to some exploring, and she wandered the ancient streets with the excitement of a child. She'd changed into blue jeans and a loose, light sweatshirt and thongs, looking as much like a tourist as the other strangers in port. Her body was still adjusting to the heat, but the sweatshirt was simply a necessity. She couldn't bear to wear form-fitting T-shirts in public. They called too much attention to her ample bustline.

She found the stalls along the waterfront particularly fascinating, and paused long enough to buy herself a sterling silver cross with inlaid mother-of-pearl. Her pidgin Spanish seemed adequate, because most of the vendors spoke a little English. Everywhere there were colorful things to see—beautiful serapes in vivid rainbow shades, ponchos, hats, straw bags and animals and sea shells. And the architecture of the old buildings near the docks fascinated her. She stared out over the bay and daydreamed about the days of pirate ships and adventure, and suddenly a picture of the big blond man flashed into her mind. Yes, he would have made a good pirate. What was it that Dutch had called pirates—freebooters? She could even picture him with a cutlass. She smiled at her own fantasy and moved on down the pier to watch some men unloading a big freighter. She'd never been around ships very much. Greenville was an inland city, far from the ocean. Mountains and rolling, unspoiled countryside were much more familiar to Dani than ships were. But she liked watching them. Lost in her daydreams, she didn't realize just how long she'd been standing there, staring. Or that her interest might seem more than casual.

One of the men on the dock began watching her, and with a feeling of uneasiness she moved back into the crowd of tourists. She didn't want trouble, and a woman alone could get into a sticky situation.

Dusk was settling over the sleepy city of Veracruz, and the man was still watching her. Out of the corner of her eye she could see him moving toward her. Oh, Lord, she thought miserably, now what do I do? She didn't see a policeman anywhere, and most of the remaining tourists were older people who wouldn't want to be dragged into someone else's problems. Dani groaned inwardly as she clutched her bag and started walking quickly toward the hotel. The crowd dispersed still farther. Now she was alone and still the footsteps sounded behind her. Her heart began to race. What if he meant to rob her? Good heavens, what if he thought she was looking for a man?

She quickened her steps and darted around a corner just as a tall form loomed up in front of her. She jerked to a stop and almost screamed before she noticed the color of his hair in the fiery sunset.

"Oh," she said weakly, one hand clutching her sweatshirt.

Dutch stared at her coolly, a cigarette in one hand, the other in his pocket. He was still wearing the khaki safari suit he'd worn on the plane, but he looked fresh and unruffled. She found herself wondering if anything could rattle him. He had an odd kind of self-confidence, as if he'd tested himself to the very limits and knew himself as few men ever did.

He glanced over her shoulder, seeming to take in the situation in one quick glance. His eyes were very dark when they met hers again. "You'll enjoy your holiday more if you keep out of this part of town after dark," he told her pleasantly enough but with authority in his tone. "You've picked up an admirer."

"Yes, I know, I..." She started to glance over her shoulder, but he shook his head.

"Don't. He'll think you're encouraging him." He laughed shortly. "He's fifty and bald," he added. "But if you purposely went down to the docks looking for a man, you might give him a wink and make his day."

He'd meant it as a joke, but the remark hurt her anyway. Clearly, he didn't think she was likely to attract a man like himself.

"It was more a case of forgetting where I was, if you want the truth. I'll know better next time. Excuse me," she said quietly, and walked past him.

He watched her go, furious with her for letting the taunt cut her, more furious with himself for not realizing that it would. He muttered something unpleasant under his breath and started after her.

But she'd had quite enough. She quickened her pace, darting into the hotel and up the staircase to the second floor instead of waiting for an elevator. She made it into her room and locked the door. Although why she should have bothered was anyone's guess. He wasn't the kind of man who chased bespectacled booksellers, she told herself coldly.

She didn't bother to go downstairs for dinner that evening. Probably he wouldn't have come near her, but she was too embarrassed to chance it. She ordered from room service, and enjoyed a seafood supper in privacy.

The next morning she went down to breakfast, too proud to let him think she was avoiding him. And sure enough, there he was, sitting alone at a window table with a newspaper. He looked good, she thought, even in nothing more unusual than white slacks and a red-and-white half-unbuttoned shirt. Just like a tourist. As if he felt her eyes on him, he lifted his gaze from the paper and caught her staring. She blushed, but he merely smiled and returned his eyes to his reading. She hardly knew what she was eating after that, and she couldn't help watching him out of the corner of one eye.

He was much too sophisticated for a little country mouse, Dani told herself sternly. She'd just have to keep well away from him. He had no interest in her, despite her helpless fascination with him. He was world-weary and cynical, and looked as if she amused him...nothing more.

She made up her mind to enjoy the rest of her four-day holiday, and went to her room, where she got out a one-piece black bathing suit to wear to the beach. She pinned her irritating hair out of the way and stared at her reflection. What ravishing good looks, she thought sarcastically. No wonder he wasn't interested. Looking the way she did, it was unlikely that even a shark would be tempted.

Go to Mexico, have fun, her friend Harriett Gaynor had said. Sparkle! Attract men! Dani sighed miserably. Back home it was spring and things were beginning to bloom, and books were selling well—especially romances. And here Dani was, with nothing changed at all except her surroundings. Alone and unloved and unwanted, as usual. She glared at herself and impulsively she called the beauty salon downstairs and made an appointment to have her hair cut.

They had a cancellation, and could take her immediately. Several minutes later she sat watching the unruly locks of hair being neatly sheared off, leaving her delicate features framed by a simple, wavy short cut that curled toward her wide eyes and gave her an impish look. She grinned at herself, pleased, and after paying the girl at the counter, she danced back upstairs and put on her bathing suit. She even added some of the makeup she never used, and perfume. The result wasn't beauty-queen glamour, but it was a definite improvement.

Then she stared at her bodice ruefully. Well, there wouldn't be any miracle to correct this problem, she told herself, and pulled on a beach wrap. It was colorful, tinted with shades of lavender, and it concealed very well. She got the beach bag she'd bought in the hotel lobby and stuffed suntan lotion and her beach towel into it. Then, with her prescription sunglasses firmly over her eyes, she set off for the beach.

It was glorious. Beach and sun and the lazy rhythm of the water all combined to relax her. She stretched, loving the beauty around her, the history of this ancient port. She wondered what the first explorers would have thought of the tourist attraction their old stomping grounds made.

Feeling as if someone were staring at her, she opened her eyes and twisted her head just a little. She saw Dutch wandering along the beach, cigarette in hand, blond head shining like white gold in the sun. He was darkly tanned, shirtless, and her fascinated eyes clung to him helplessly. He wasn't a hairy man, but there was a wedge of curling dark blond hair over the darkly tanned muscles of his chest and stomach. His legs were feathered with it, too, long, powerful legs in cutoff denim shorts, and he wore thongs, as most of the people on the beach did, to protect against unexpected objects in the sand.

She turned her head away so that she didn't have to see him. He was a sensuous man, devastating to a woman who knew next to nothing about the male sex. He had to be aware of her naivete, and it probably amused him, she thought bitterly.

He watched her head turn, and irritation flashed in his dark eyes. Why was she always gazing at him with that helpless-child longing? She disturbed him. His eyes narrowed. New haircut, wasn't it? The haircut suited her, but why in hell was she wrapped up like a newly caught fish? He'd yet to see her in anything that didn't cover her from neck to waist. He frowned. Probably she was flat-chested and didn't want to call attention to it. But didn't she realize that her attempts at camouflage were only pointing out her shortcoming?

He glowered at her. Long legs, nice legs, he mused, narrowing his eyes as he studied the relaxed body on the giant beach towel. Nice hips, too. Flat, very smooth lines. Tiny waist. But then there was the coverup. She'd said she needed to lose weight, but he couldn't imagine where. She looked perfect to him.

She was just a woman, he thought, pulling himself up. Just another faithless flirt, out for what she could get. Would he never learn? Hadn't he paid for his one great love affair already? Love affair, he thought bitterly. Never that. An infatuation that had cost him everything he held dear. His home, his future, the savings his parents had sacrificed to give him...

He tore his eyes away and turned them seaward. Sometimes it got the better of him. It had no part of the present. In fact, neither did Miss Frump over there.

He turned, blatantly staring at her, a tiny smile playing around his mouth. She was a different species of woman, unfamiliar to him. He found he was curious about her, about what made her tick.

He moved forward slowly, and she saw him out of the corner of her eye. She felt her pulse exploding as he came closer. No, she pleaded silently, closing her eyes. Please, go away. Don't encourage me. Don't come near me. You make me vulnerable, and that's the one thing I mustn't be.

"You won't get much sun in that," he remarked, indicating the top as he plopped down beside her. He leaned on an elbow, stretched full-length beside her, and she could feel the heat of him, smell the cologne that clung to him.

"I don't want to burn," she said in a strangled tone.

"Still angry about what I said last night?" he asked on a smile.

"A little, yes," she said honestly.

He leaned over and tugged her sunglasses away from her eyes so that they were naked and vulnerable. He was worldly and it showed, and so did her fear of him.

"I didn't mean to ridicule you. I'm not used to women," he said bluntly. "I've lived a long time without them."

"And you don't like them, either," she said perceptively.

He scowled briefly, letting his eyes drop to her mouth. "Occasionally. In bed." He chuckled softly at her telltale color. "Don't tell me I embarrass you? Not considering the type of reading material you carry around with you. Surely every detail is there in black and white."

"Not the way you're thinking," she protested.

"Little southern lady," he murmured, watching her. She had a softness that he wasn't used to, a vulnerability. But there was steel under it. He sensed a spirit as strong as his own beneath shyness. "Do I frighten you?"

"Yes. I...don't have much to do with men," she said quietly. "And I'm not very worldly."

"Are you always that honest?" he asked absently as he studied her nose. There were a few scattered freckles on its bridge.

"I don't like being lied to," she said. "So I try very hard not to lie to other people."

"The golden rule?" He fingered a short strand of her brown hair, noticing the way it shone in the sunlight, as sleek as mink, silky in his hand. "I like your haircut."

"It was hot having it long..." She faltered. She wasn't used to being touched, and there was something magnetic about this man. It was unsettling to have so much vibrant masculinity so close that she could have run her hands over his body. He made her feel things she hadn't experienced since her teens, innocent longings that made her tense with mingled fear and need.

"Why are you wearing this?" he asked, and his hand went to the buttons of her shapeless overblouse. "Do you really need it?"

She could hardly swallow. He had her so rattled, she didn't know her name. "I...no, but..." she began.

"Then take it off," he said quietly. "I want to see what you look like."

There had been a similar passage in the latest book by her favorite author. She'd read it and gotten breathless. But this was real, and the look in his dark eyes made her tremble. She forgot why she was wearing the wrap and watched his hard face as he eased the buttons skillfully out of their holes and finally drew the garment from around her body.

His breath caught audibly. He seemed to stop breathing as he looked down on what he'd uncovered. "My God," he whispered.

She was blushing again, feeling like a nervous adolescent.

"Why?" he asked, meeting her eyes.

She shifted restlessly. "Well, I'm. . .I feel...men stare," she finished miserably.

"My God, of course they stare! You're exquisite!"

She's never heard it put that way. She searched his eyes, looking for ridicule, but there was none. He was staring again, and she found that a part of her she didn't recognize liked the way he was looking at her.

"Is that why you wear bulky tops all the time?" he persisted gently.

She sighed. "Men seem to think that women who are...well-endowed have loose morals. It's embarrassing to be stared at."

"I thought you were flat-chested," he mused, laughing.

"Well, no, I'm not," she managed. "I guess I did look rather odd."

He smiled down at her. "Leave it off," he said with a last lingering scrutiny before he stretched out on his back. "I'll fend off unwanted admirers for you."

She was immediately flattered. And nervous. Would he expect any privileges for that protection? She stared at his relaxed body uneasily.

"No strings," he murmured, eyes closed. "I want rest, not a wild, hot affair."

She sighed. "Just as well," she said ruefully. "I wouldn't know how to have one."

"Are you a virgin?" he asked matter-of-factly.

"Yes."

"Unusual these days."

"I believe in happily-ever-after."

"Yes, I could tell by your reading material," he said with a lazy smile. He stretched, and powerful muscles rippled all up and down his tanned body. Her gaze was drawn to it, held by it.

He opened his eyes and watched her, oddly touched by the rapt look on her young face. He'd have bet a year's earnings that she'd never been touched even in the most innocent way. He found himself wondering what she might be like in passion, whether those pale eyes would glow, whether her body would relax and trust his. He frowned slightly. He'd never taken time with a woman, not since that she-wolf. These days it was all quickly over and forgotten. But slow, tender wooing was something he could still remember. And suddenly he felt a need for it. To touch this silky creature next to him and teach her how to love. How to touch. The thought of her long fingers on him caused a sudden and shocking reaction in his body.

He turned over onto his stomach, half-dazed with the unexpected hunger. Was she a witch? He studied her. Did she know what had happened to him? No, he decided, if she did, it would be highly visible in those virginal cheeks. She probably didn't even know what happened to men at all. He smiled slowly at the searching wonder in her eyes.

"Why are you smiling like that?" she asked softly.

"Do you really want to know?" he murmured dryly.

She rolled over onto her stomach as well, and propped herself up on her elbows, looking down at him, at the hard lines of his face, the faint scarring on one cheek. She felt drawn to him physically, and couldn't understand why it seemed so natural to lie beside him and look at him.

His eyes were fixed on a sudden parting of fabric that gave a tantalizing view of her generous breasts, and when she started to move, he reached up and held her still.

"You won't get pregnant if I look at you," he whispered.

"You're a horrible man," she said haughtily.

"Yes, but I'm much safer than any one of these wily Latins," he told her. "The lesser of two evils, you might say. I won't seduce you."

"As if any man would want to." She laughed, and started to move away again. This time he let her, looming over her as she lay back, with his forearms beside her head and his eyes boring into hers at close range.

"If we weren't on a public beach, I'd give you a crash course in arousal, doubting Thomasina," he murmured. "Something just happened to me that shocked me to the back teeth, and it's your fault."

Her eyes widened as her mind tried to convince her that she hadn't heard him make such a blatant statement.

"I see you understand me," he said with a lazy smile. "What's wrong, southern belle, have you led such a sheltered life?"

She swallowed. "Yes." She studied his hard face. "Yours hasn't been sheltered."

"That's right," he told her. "I could turn your hair white with the story of my life. Especially," he added deliberately, unblinkingly, "the part of it that concerns women."

Her eyes dilated as they held his. "You...aren't a romantic."

He shook his head slowly. "No," he said quietly. "Occasionally I need a woman, the oblivion of sex. But that's all it ever is. Sex, with no illusions."

Her eyes searched his, reading embarrassing things in them. "There's a reason," she said softly, knowingly.

He nodded. "I was twenty-four. She was twenty-eight, wildly experienced, and as beautiful as a goddess. She seduced me on the deck of a yacht, and after that I'd have died for her. But she was expensive, and I was besotted, and eventually I sold everything I had to buy her loyalty." His eyes darkened, went cold with memory and rage as Dani watched. "I'd helped buy my parents a small home for their retirement with money I...earned," he added, not mentioning how he'd earned the money. "And I even mortgaged that. The bank foreclosed. My father, who'd put his life savings into his part of the house, died of a heart attack soon afterward. My mother blamed me for it, for taking away the thing he'd worked all his life for. She died six months later."

He'd picked up a handful of sand and was letting it fall slowly onto the beach while she stared at his handsome profile and knew somehow that he'd never told this story to another living soul.

"And the woman?" she asked gently.

The sand made a small sound, and his palm flattened on it, crushing it. "She found another chump..." He glanced at Dani with a cold laugh. "One with more money."

"I'm sorry," she said inadequately. "I can understand that it would have made you bitter. But—"

"But all women aren't cold-hearted cheats?" he finished for her, glaring. "Aren't they?"

"The one boyfriend I ever had was two-timing me with another girl," she said.

"What a blazing affair it must have been," he said with cold sarcasm.

She searched his face, seeing beneath the anger to the pain. "I loved him," she said with a gentle smile. "But he was more interested in physical satisfaction than undying devotion."

"Most men are," he said curtly.

"I suppose so." She sighed. She rolled over onto her back and stretched. "I've decided that I like being alone, anyway. It's a lot safer."

He eased onto his side, watching her. "You disturb me," he said after a minute.

"Why? Because I'm not experienced?" she asked.

He nodded. "My world doesn't cater to inexperience. You're something of a curiosity to me."

"Yes. So are you, to me," she confessed, studying him blatantly.

He brushed the hair away from her face with strong, warm hands, callused hands that felt as if he'd used them in hard work. She liked that roughness against her soft skin. It made her tingle and ache with pleasure. He looked down at the bodice of the bathing suit, watching her reaction. The material was thin and the hard tips of her breasts were as evident as her quickened breathing.

She started to move her arms, to cover herself, but he caught her eyes and shook his head.

"That's as natural as breathing," he said in a voice that barely carried above the sound of the surf. "It's very flattering. Don't be ashamed of it."

"I was raised by a maiden aunt," she told him. "She never married, and I was taught that—"

He pressed his thumb over her mouth, a delicious contact that made her want to bite it gently. "I can imagine what you were taught." He let his dark gaze drop to her mouth and studied it slowly as he touched it, watching it tremble and part. "I like your mouth, Dani. I'd like to take it with mine."

The thought was exciting, wildly exciting. Her gaze went involuntarily to his hard, chiseled mouth. His upper lip was thin, the bottom one wide and sensuous. She would bet he'd forgotten more about kissing than she'd ever learned.

"Have you been kissed very much?" he asked.

"Once or twice," she said lightly, trying to joke.

"French kisses?" he provoked.

Her body was going crazy. She could feel her heart trying to escape her chest, and her breathing was audible. It got even worse when his hard fingers left her mouth to run down the side of her neck, across her collarbone and, incredibly, onto the swell of her breast above the swimsuit.

Her gasp whispered against his lips and he smiled. "Shocking, isn't it?" he murmured, watching her eyes dilate, her face flush as his fingers lazily slid under the strap. His body shielded her from other sunbathers, and there was no one in front of them. "No one can see us," he whispered reassuringly. He laughed softly, wickedly, as his fingers slid under the fabric with a lazy teasing pressure that was more provocative than frightening. Her body reacted wildly to being teased, and she knew that he could see what was happening. He was much too sophisticated not to know exactly what she was feeling.

"Skin like warm silk," he breathed, his mouth poised just above hers while his fingers brushed her like whispers of sensation, and she tensed and trembled as the pleasure began to grow.

She wanted more. She wanted him to touch the hard, aching tip of her breasts; she wanted to watch him do it, to see him possess her with that callused, expert hand. Her face even told him so.

His eyes were getting darker now, and the indulgent smile was vanishing as well. "If you keep looking at me like that," he said under his breath, "I'm going to slide my hand completely over you and to hell with spectators."

Her lips parted. She felt reckless and abandoned and vulnerable. Four days in which to store a lifetime of memories, she thought bitterly. Every one of her friends was married, every one of them had some happiness. But not Dani. Not ever. And now this man, who could have had any woman on the beach, was playing with her, amusing himself, because he saw how vulnerable she was...and she was letting him.

Her eyes clouded, and something deep inside the blond man stirred helplessly when he saw it.

"No," he whispered with aching tenderness. "Don't. I'm not playing."

She bit her lower lip to stop sudden tears. He saw so much, for a stranger. "Yes, you are," she protested. "You—"

His mouth lowered onto hers, just enough to let her lips experience its texture before he withdrew it. His hand, resting warmly under the strap of her bathing suit, began to move.

Her body trembled, and he whispered, "Hush," brushing his mouth tenderly over the bridge of her nose. "No one can see what I'm going to do to you." His lips went to her eyes, brushing them tenderly closed. His long fingers nudged under the fabric, farther and farther.

Her hands were on his shoulders, her fingers clinging, her breath sighing out unsteadily against his tormenting mouth. "Eric," she whispered experimentally.

He hesitated for an instant, lifting his blond head. He looked down into eyes that were full of new sensations, wide and soft and hazy. His free hand eased to the back of her neck, stroking it softly. He held her gaze as his hand moved slowly down, and then up, and she felt the warm roughness of his palm against the hard point of her breast.

"Is this the first time?" he whispered.

"Can't you...tell?" she whispered back brokenly. Her body moved helplessly, so that she could experience every texture of his hand where it rested, and an odd, tearful smile touched her mouth. "Thank you. Thank..."

He couldn't bear it. The gratitude hurt him. He moved his hand back up to her face and kissed her mouth softly, with a tenderness he hadn't shown any woman since he was little more than a boy.

"You speak as if you think it's a hardship for me just to touch you," he said quietly. "If you knew more about men, you might realize that I'm as aroused by you as you are by me."

"Me?" she repeated, her eyes wide and bright and full of magic.

"You, you voluptuous, exciting little virgin," he said, his voice rough with laughter. "I ache all over."

She began to smile, and his attention was caught by the sunniness of it, by the sudden beauty of her face. And he'd thought her drab and dull. How odd. He sensed a deeply buried sensuality in that voluptuous body, and he wanted it.

He propped himself up on an elbow, his free hand still tugging absently at her short hair.

She gave her eyes the freedom to roam that powerful body, talking in its bronzed sensuousness, the light covering of dark blond hair on his chest, his rippling stomach muscles, his strongly muscled thighs. He even had nice feet. And his legs weren't pale, as most American men's were. They were broad and dark, and looked good.

"I like your legs, too," he murmured.

She glanced back up. "Do you mind?" she asked gently. "I know I'm gawking like a schoolgirl."

"You're very honest, aren't you?" he remarked for the second time that day. "It's vaguely disconcerting. No, I don't mind if you look at me. Except that it—"

"It...?" she persisted.

"Arouses me," he said frankly.

"Just to be looked at?" she asked, fascinated.

He smiled a little. "Maybe it's my age," he said with a shrug. "You have very expressive eyes, did you know? They tell me everything you're thinking."

"Do they really?" She laughed, looking up at him. "What am I thinking now?" she asked, her mind carefully blank.

He pursed his lips and smiled slowly, and she felt a deep, slow ache in her body that was intensified when she looked at the broad sweep of his chest.

"That you'd like to have dinner with me," he hedged. "How about it?"

"Yes. I'd like to. If you won't seduce me for dessert," she added.

He sighed softly. "I'd like to have you," he confessed. "But I couldn't quite take you in my stride, either. A virgin would be something of a rarity for me. Most of my one-night stands have been the exact opposite of virgins."

She tried not to blush, but her cheeks betrayed her.

He searched her eyes. "I wouldn't hurt you," he said suddenly. "And with you, it would have to be lovemaking, not sex."

Her body felt boneless as he searched her eyes, and there was a flash of something like tenderness in the look he gave her. "I'm sorry," she said.

"Why?"

She dropped her eyes to his chest. "Because I think...I'd have liked you...for a lover."

"Yes, I think I'd have liked you for one," he agreed softly. He tilted her face back to his and searched her eyes. "Wrong time, wrong place. We should have met ten years ago."

She smiled ruefully. "You wouldn't have liked me at sixteen," she said. "I really was twenty pounds overweight."

He drew in a slow breath. "And I was in the early days of some pretty raw living," he agreed. "What a pity." He lifted her hand and kissed the soft palm, watching her face color with pleasure. "How long will you be here?"

"Four days," she said miserably.

His teeth bit into the soft flesh. "Make some memories with me," he whispered.

"That will only make it worse..." she began.

"We'll keep it light," he said. "I won't seduce you."

"By tomorrow I'll probably beg you to," she said unhappily, studying him with helpless longing. "I'm frighteningly vulnerable with you."

His eyes went along her body and he felt himself going rigid with desire. "Yes. I'm pretty vulnerable myself."

She had to force her eyes to stay on his face, and he smiled wickedly, knowing exactly what she was thinking.

He laughed and she rolled over onto her stomach again.

"Don't worry," he murmured as he stretched out beside her. "I'll take care of you. Don't sweat it."

She turned her eyes toward his and searched them, and then she smiled. "You're so handsome," she whispered helplessly.

"You're a knockout yourself," he said. "Flat-chested, hell." He laughed. "You're dynamite!"

"Thank you."

He searched her face appreciatively. "So innocent. J.D. would laugh himself sick at me."

"J.D.?" she asked curiously.

"An old friend." He grinned. "Close your eyes and let's soak up some sun. Later, I'll take you sightseeing." His eyes closed and then opened. "Not to the docks," he added, and closed them again.

She closed her own eyes with a smile. Miracles, she thought wistfully, did occasionally happen to lonely spinsters. These were going to be the four most beautiful days of her entire life. She wouldn't take a second of them for granted, starting now.

Three

Dani was glad she'd stopped by the little bou-
tique in the basement of the hotel on her way up to
change for dinner. She'd bought a white Mexican
dress with an elastic neckline and lots of ruffles,
and when she put it on she looked slightly mysterious, with her brown hair and gray eyes and
creamy complexion. Her wire-rimmed glasses
weren't so spiffy, she admitted, but they did make
her eyes look bigger than they were. And she
wasn't really fat, she told herself, smiling at her
reflection. It was mostly what was on top, and the
dress even minimized that. She got her small evening bag and went downstairs to meet Dutch in the
lobby.

He was wearing white slacks with a white shirt
and blue blazer, and he rose lazily to his feet from

a plush sofa, leaving his evening paper there as he joined her.

"Nice," he said, taking her arm. "What do you fancy? Mexican, Chinese, Italian, or a steak?"

"I like steak," she murmured.

"So do I." He guided her along the hall past the family restaurant and into the very exclusive Captain's Quarters next door. White-coated waiters in white gloves were everywhere, and Dani glanced up at Dutch apprehensively as he gave the hostess his name.

"What is it?" he asked softly, guiding her along behind the well-dressed young woman with the menus.

"It's so expensive," she began, worried.

His face brightened, and he smiled. "Do you mind washing dishes afterward?" he whispered mischievously.

She laughed up at him. "Not if you'll dry," she promised.

He slid an arm around her waist and pulled her close. "You're a nice girl."

"Just the kind your mother warned you about, so look out," she told him.

He glanced down at her. "No. My mother would have liked you. She was spirited, too."

She smiled shyly, aware of envious eyes following them along the way. He was so handsome, she thought, peeking up at him. Muscular, graceful, and with the face of a Greek statue, male perfection in the finest sense. An artist would have been enchanted with him as a subject.

The hostess left them at their table, near the window, and Dutch seated Dani with a curious frown.

"What were you thinking about so solemnly just now?" he asked as he eased his tall form into the chair across from her.

"That you'd delight an artist," she said simply. "You're very elegant."

He took a slow breath. "Lady, you're bad for my ego."

"Surely you look in the mirror from time to time?" she asked. "I don't mean to stare, but I can't help it."

"Yes, I have the same problem," he murmured, and his eyes were fixed on her.

She was glad she hadn't yielded to the temptation to pull the elastic neck of her dress down around her shoulders. It was hard enough to bear that dark stare as it was.

"Shall I order for you, or are you liberated?" he asked after she'd studied the menu.

"I kind of like it the old-fashioned way, if you don't mind," she confessed. "I'm liberated enough to know I look better in a skirt than in a pair of pants."

He chuckled. "Do you?"

"Well, you'd look pretty silly in a dress," she came back.

"What do you want to eat?" he asked.

"Steak and a salad and coffee to drink."

He looked at her with a dry smile, and when the waiter came, he gave a double order.

"Yes," he told her, "I like coffee, too."

"You seem very traveled," she remarked, pleating her napkin.

"I am." He leaned back in his chair to study her. "And you've never been out of the States."

"I've been nowhere—until now." She smiled at the napkin. "Done nothing except work. I thought about changing, but I never had the courage to do it."

"It takes courage, to break out of a mold," he said. He pulled the ashtray toward him and lit a cigarette. "I hope you don't mind, but I'm doing it anyway. This is one habit I don't intend to break."

" 'I'll die of something someday,' " she quoted. "There are lots of other clichés, but I think that one's dandy."

He only laughed. "Smoking is the least dangerous thing I do."

"What *do* you do?" she asked, curious.

He thought about that for a moment, and pursed his lips as he wondered what she'd say if he told her the truth. She'd probably be out of that chair and out of his life so fast... He frowned. He didn't like that idea.

"I'm in the military," he said finally. "In a sense."

"Oh. On active duty?" she continued, feeling her way because he seemed reluctant to elaborate.

"No. Inactive, at the moment." He watched her through a veil of smoke from his cigarette.

"Is it dangerous, what you do?"

"Yes."

"I feel like a panelist on 'What's My Line?' " she said unexpectedly, and grinned when he burst out laughing.

"Maybe you're a double agent," she supposed. "A spy."

"I'm too tall," he returned. "Agents are supposed to be under five feet tall so that they can hide in shrubbery."

She stared at him until she realized he was joking, and she laughed.

"Your eyes laugh when you do," he said absently. "Are you always this sunny?"

"Most of the time," she confessed. She pushed her glasses back as they threatened to slide down her nose. "I have my bad days, too, like everyone else, but I try to leave them at home."

"You could get contact lenses," he remarked as he noticed her efforts to keep her glasses on her nose.

She shook her head. "I'm much too nervous to be putting them in and taking them out and putting them in solution all the time. I'm used to these."

"They must get in the way when you kiss a man," he murmured dryly.

"What way?" She laughed, a little embarrassed by his frankness. "My life isn't overrun with amorous men."

"We can take them off, I suppose," he mused.

Her breath caught as she read the veiled promise in his dark eyes.

"Stark terror," he taunted gently, watching her expression. "I didn't realize I was so frightening."

"Not that kind of frightening," she corrected him. Her eyes lowered.

"Dani."

He made her name sound like a prayer. She looked up.

"Seducing you is not on the agenda," he said quietly. "But if something did happen, I'd marry you. That's a promise, and I don't give my word lightly."

She began to tingle all over. "It would be a high price to pay for one mistake."

He was watching her oddly. "Would it? I haven't thought about marriage in years." He leaned back in his chair to study her, the cigarette burning idly in his fingers. "I wonder what it would be like," he mused, "having someone to come back to."

What an odd way to put it, she thought. Surely he meant someone to come *home* to. She pulled herself up short as she realized that it was just conversation. He was only amusing himself; she had to remember that. Making memories, as he'd put it. They were strangers and they'd remain strangers. She couldn't afford to mess up her whole life because of a holiday romance. That was all this was. A little light entertainment. She'd better remember that, too.

The waiter brought their food, and as they ate they talked about general things. He seemed very knowledgeable about foreign conflicts, and she imagined that he read a lot of military publications. That led to talk of the kind of weapons being used, and he seemed equally knowledgeable about those.

"My best friend's husband likes to read about weapons," Dani volunteered, remembering Harriett's Dave and his fascination with weaponry. "He has volumes on those exotic things like...oh, what is it, the little nine-millimeter carbine—"

"The Uzi," he offered. "It has a thirty-shot magazine and can throw off single shots as well as bursts. A formidable little carbine."

She laughed. "I can shoot a twenty-two rifle. That's about the extent of my knowledge of weapons."

"I know more about knives than guns, as a rule, although I've used both." He reached into his inside blazer pocket, produced a large folded knife and put it on the table.

She stared at it, fascinated. It was made of silvery metal, with a carved bone handle, and when she tugged the blade out, it was oddly shaped and had a sinister look.

"It's not a pocket knife, is it?" she asked, lifting her eyes.

He shook his head. "Although it passes for one, going through customs."

"Where did you find something so unusual?" she asked, fascinated by it.

"I made it." He picked it up and repocketed it.

"Made it?" she exclaimed.

"Sure." He laughed at her expression. "Where do you think knives come from? Someone has to make them."

"Yes, of course, but I didn't recognize... It's very formidable looking," she added.

"I don't carry it for decoration," he said. He leaned forward and sipped his coffee. "Would you like some dessert?"

"No, thank you," she said. "I don't like sweet things very much, thank God."

He smiled. "Neither do I. Let's go walk on the beach for a while."

"Lovely!"

She waited while he paid the check and then followed him out into the darkness.

The night was warm, and she took off her sandals, which she'd worn without hose, and danced in and out of the waves. He watched her, laughing, his hands in his pockets, his blond hair pale and glowing in the light from the hotel.

"How old did you say you were?" he asked when she came running back up the beach, sandals dangling from one hand.

"About ten," she laughed up at him.

"You make me feel old." He lifted a hand and touched her cheek, her lips. There were people farther down the beach, but none close enough to be more than dark shapes.

"How old are you?" she asked.

"Thirty-six," he said. His other hand came out of his pocket. He took her sandals from her nerveless fingers and dropped them down into the sand. The soft thud barely registered above the crashing surf.

"You excite me," he said in a deep, slow tone. He cupped her face in his hands and drew her closer, so that she could feel the pleasant heat of his body against hers. "Do you know how a man's body reacts when he's excited?"

Her face felt blistering hot, and she couldn't seem to move as he released her face only to take her hips in his hands and draw them against him.

Her breath caught and his open mouth touched her forehead. His breathing was audible now, and she was learning fascinating things about him, about the subtle differences in his body that she was apparently causing.

"No protest at all?" he asked quietly.

"I'm...curious," she whispered. "As you've already seen, I know very little about this."

"I don't frighten you?"

"No, not now."

His mouth smiled, she could feel it. His thumbs bit into the soft flesh of her stomach as he urged her closer. "Not even now?" he whispered.

Her legs trembled against his. She felt strange new sensations inside her, dragging sensations that left tingling pleasure in their wake. Her hands clung to his blazer because she wasn't sure her legs were going to support her much longer.

His chest rose and fell roughly against her taut breasts. "I want to be alone with you. And at the moment that's the most dangerous thing we could do."

"You want me," she whispered, realizing it with a strange sense of triumph.

"Yes." His hands moved up her body slowly to her breasts, which were bare under the dress because she hadn't wanted to suffer her hot, long-line bra, which was the only strapless thing she had.

She tensed, feeling his hands lift her, cup her, so tender that she accepted them without protest. His thumbs brushed over her, feeling her instant response.

"You want me, too, don't you?" he asked gently.

The sensations his thumbs were producing made her mind go blank. She moved a little, moaning.

His face pressed against her cheek. She could feel his breath at her ear.

"Thank God we don't have an audience," he whispered huskily. "Stand very still, Dani."

His hands rose, moved to her shoulders. He eased the fabric down her arms with a slow, sinuous, achingly tender pressure. Her heart stopped beating as she felt the blood rush through her veins, felt the coolness of the salty night breeze touching her shoulders, her upper arms, and then her breasts as he slid the fabric to her waist.

She moaned again, a catching of breath that acted on him like a narcotic. He felt his own legs go weak at the wholehearted response she was giving him. Giving to him, when he knew instinctively that she'd never have let any other man do this to her.

"I wish that I could see your eyes," he whispered. He lifted his head and looked down at her shadowed face. His hands slid against her face, her throat. "You're so silky-soft," he said under his breath. His hands slid down her arms and back up, his fingers barely touching, experiencing her skin. "Like warm cream. I can feel you trembling, and it brings the blood to my head, did you know? And that little sound you made when I pulled your dress away from your breasts..." His hands moved back to her shoulders. "Sweet, sweet virgin," he whispered. "Make it easy for me. Lift your arms and let me hold you in my palms."

She stood on tiptoe as his hands began to move over her collarbone. Her hands reached up into his thick, straight blond hair as his thumbs moved down ahead of his palms and rubbed sensually at the hard tips of her breasts.

She jerked helplessly at the exquisite contact.

"I want to put my mouth on you," he whispered as his lips brushed hers and his hands slowly, achingly, swallowed her, feeling the involuntary tremors that shook her. "All of this is a natural part of lovemaking, so don't be frightened if you feel my teeth. All right?"

"Peo-ple," she moaned helplessly.

"There was only an old couple down the beach," he whispered. "They've gone inside now. Dani, Dani, of all the erotic, unbelievably sexy things I've ever done with a woman, this has to be the sweetest!"

She was arching her body toward him, blind and deaf to everything except sensation. Tomorrow, she told her conscience, tomorrow I'll worry about it.

"You want my mouth, don't you, darling?" he said, and with something like reverence he began to run his lips along her throat, down the side of her neck, over her collarbone, her shoulders. "I'm going to make a meal of you right here," he breathed, and all at once she felt his teeth on her and she stiffened and cried out.

"Eric," she moaned, frightened, her hands catching in his hair.

"It's all right," he murmured against her breast. "I wouldn't hurt you for all the world. Relax, darling, just relax. Yes, like that, Dani. Lie down. Lie down, so that I can get to you...."

He was easing her down onto the sand, and she let him, grateful to have some support under her, because the world was spinning around wildly. She clung to him, glorying in the feel of his lips, his teeth, his tongue, as he showed her how inexperienced she really was. By the time he got back to her mouth she was on fire for him.

With fierce enthusiasm she pulled his body down over hers and kissed him back with a naive but satisfying passion. He laughed delightedly against her open mouth and eased his hips over hers. She was his already.

"Eric," she ventured shakily.

"What do you want?" he asked, tasting her closed eyelids.

Her hands went to the front of his shirt, and he lifted his head. "Do you want to feel me?"

She flushed. "Yes."

"Unbutton it."

He was heavy, but she loved his weight. Overhead there were hundreds of stars. But all she knew was the unexpected completeness of his passion.

She touched his bare, hair-rough skin with hands that tingled with excitement. She'd never touched a man's body before, but she loved the feel of Dutch's. His muscles were padded, warm and strong, and she could imagine that his strength was formidable.

"Move your hands," he said seconds later, and when she did, he dragged his bare chest roughly over hers, shocking her with the force of desire the unexpected action caused in her body.

"Do you like it?" he asked as he moved sinuously above her.

"I never dreamed..." she began huskily. She was trembling, and so was her voice. "Oh, I want you," she confessed on a sob. "I want you, I want you!"

"I want you, too, little one," he whispered, kissing her softly. "But I can't treat you like a one-night stand. I find I have too much conscience."

Tears were rolling down her cheeks. He kissed them all away, and his tongue brushed the tears from her eyelashes, and she realized suddenly that she hadn't had her glasses on for quite a while.

"My...glasses?" she falterd.

"Above your head," he said with a smile. He sat up slowly, catching her wrists to pull her up with him. She was in a patch of light that allowed him a delicious view of creamy, hard-tipped breasts in blatant arousal.

"Oh, you're something else, Miss St. Clair," he said gently. He bent and touched his mouth to the very tip of one breast.

Her breath wouldn't come steadily. She looked down at his blond head. "I...we should...that is..."

He lifted his head. "Suppose in the morning we get married?"

"M-married?"

He nodded. "Married." He pulled up her bodice with obvious reluctance. Then he reached behind her, retrieved her glasses, and put them back on her.

"But..."

His knuckles brushed one perfect breast lazily, feeling it go hard again. "This isn't going to get better," he said. "By tomorrow we'll be in such a fever that nothing is going to keep us away from each other. I haven't experienced anything this powerful since I was about fifteen. And I'm damned sure you're feeling it for the first time."

"Yes, I know that, but we're strangers," she protested, trying to keep her head.

"We aren't going to be strangers for much longer," he said flatly. "My God, I want you," he ground out. "If you won't marry me, I'm getting the hell out of this hotel tonight, and on the next plane out of Veracruz. Because I can't bear to be around you without taking you. And I won't take you without marriage."

"But..."

"Am I so unmarriageable?" he burst out. "My God, I've had women propose to *me*! I'm not ugly, I'm well to do, I like dogs and cats, and I pay my bills on time. I'm in fairly decent health, I have friends...why in hell won't you marry me?"

"But it's only desire," she began.

"Stop trying to be logical," he said gruffly. "I'm not capable of logic when I'm aching like this. I want you. And you want me. For God's sake, put me out of my misery!"

"Would...would we have a divorce if...after we...if you..." she began.

"I'm getting older." He got to his feet and drew her up with him. "I travel a lot, you'd have to get used to that. But until now I've never had anyone of my own. I like you. I like being with you. And I think we'll set fires in bed. It's more than most people start out with. At least we aren't kids who believe in fairy tales like love and happily-ever-after. I'd rather have a woman who doesn't bore me than an infatuation that wears off."

"And if you fell in love with someone later?" she asked quietly, hearing her dreams die.

"I'll never love again," he said with equal quietness. "But if you do, I'll let you out." He took her hands in his. "Yes or no? I won't ask again."

"Yes," she said without hesitation. Harriett would faint. Nobody would believe it back home, that she'd found a man like this who wanted her. All the questions she'd meant to ask went right out of her mind.

He bent and kissed her—without passion and very tenderly. "My full name is Eric James van Meer. I was born in the Netherlands, although everyone calls it Holland, in a place called Utrecht. I lived there until I was in my teens, when I joined the service. The rest, you know, a little. Someday I'll tell you all of it. When I have to."

"That sounds ominous."

He put an arm around her. "It doesn't have a lot to do with us right now," he said. His arm tightened. "Do you want to be a virgin until tomorrow morning?"

Her lips parted. Her breath came wildly. Of course, she thought, and started to say it. But she couldn't. The words stuck in her throat. She thought of the long night, and her logical mind was booted out of its lofty position by a body that was in unholy torment.

"I want you so much," she said unsteadily.

"No more than I want you," he returned gruffly.

They were in the light of the hotel lobby now. He stopped, turning her toward him. His hands cupped her face and his eyes were dark and hot and full of anguish.

"I was raised a Catholic," he explained. "And in my religion, what I'm going to do to you tonight is a sin. Probably in your religion it is, too. But in the sight of God, for all our lives, I take you for my wife here, now. And tomorrow, in the sight of men, we make it right."

Tears stung her eyes as the words touched her heart. "And I take you for my husband, for better or worse, as long as I draw breath."

He bent and brushed his mouth tenderly over her wet eyes. "In Dutch, we call a married woman *Mevrouw*," he whispered.

"*Mevrouw*," she repeated.

"And darling," he added, smiling, "is *lieveling*."

"*Lieveling*," she repeated, smiling back.

"Upstairs," he said, turning her, "I'll teach you some more words. But you won't be able to repeat them in public." And he laughed at her expression.

Four

Dutch's room was nothing like Dani's. It overlooked the bay, and its quiet elegance would have suited royalty. She watched him lock the door, and nervously went to stand on the balcony where she could see a lighted ship in port.

The wind blew her hair and her dress, and she felt like a voyager on the brink of a new discovery.

"One of the passenger ships," he remarked, nodding toward the brilliantly lighted vessel. "Beautiful, isn't she?"

"Yes. I don't know much about ships, but I like looking at them."

He lit a cigarette and smoked it quietly. "I used to sail," he said unexpectedly.

She turned, looking up at the stranger who, in less than twenty-four hours, would be her husband and her lover. "Did you?"

"I moved to Chicago about eight years ago," he said. "I have an apartment on the lake, and I had a sailboat. I got drunk one night and she turned over with me. I let her sink."

Her eyes narrowed uneasily as she stared up at him, and he stared back, unblinkingly.

"I'm not an alcoholic," he said gently. "I probably sound like one to you, with these veiled references to the past. I don't drink often, but there are times when I get black moods. I won't drink around you. Ever."

It sounded as if he were willing to make any compromise, and something warm and soft blossomed inside her. She went close to him, her eyes trusting, quiet and deep. "I can make compromises, too," she said quietly. "I'll live anywhere you like."

He searched her eyes. "I don't mind readjusting."

"Yes, I know, but your work is in Chicago, I gather, or you wouldn't live there."

"My work is international," he said, and scowled. "I don't work out of Chicago. I live there because I have friends there."

"Women friends?" she blurted out.

He only smiled. He finished the cigarette, tossed it into an ashtray and drew her gently against him. "You're going to be the first woman I've spent time with this year," he murmured with a mocking smile. "Does that answer the question?"

She felt and looked shocked. "But...but don't you need...?" She couldn't find a delicate way to say it.

"I thought I was beyond all that, until you came along," he confessed. "I can't even remember the last time I felt this way about a woman."

"Are you sure you want to marry me?" she asked.

"Don't worry so," he told her, bending to kiss away the frown. "Yes, I want to marry you. I'll still want to marry you in the morning, too. That was no lie to get you in bed with me."

Part of her had thought that, and she lowered her eyes to his collar.

"Second thoughts?" he asked.

Her fingers toyed with the buttons on his shirt. "I'm afraid."

"Yes, I imagine so," he said matter-of-factly. "The first time was hard for me, too. I was nervous as a cat." He laughed.

"I can't imagine you being nervous," she said.

"It was forever ago. But I haven't forgotten. I'll go slowly." He bent and touched her mouth with his, very gently. "I just want you to remember two things. The first is that there are no set rules in this—it all depends on what pleases the people involved. Will you try to keep that in mind?"

She swallowed. "Yes."

"The second thing is that I'm not superhuman," he said softly. "Inevitably, there will come a moment when I lose control absolutely. Hopefully, I can bring you to that point before I reach it. But if not, I'll make it up to you afterward. Okay?"

"It all seems so mysterious," she whispered, as if even the night had ears.

"It won't by morning." His gaze went slowly over her, from head to toe and back up again, and his breathing began to change. "Rosebud," he muttered softly as he suddenly swung her up into his hard arms.

She relaxed a little and burrowed her face into his warm throat. He smelled of expensive cologne, and she loved the strength that made her seem so light in his embrace.

He laid her down on the bed gently. She expected him to start undressing himself or her immediately, and she lay there uneasily, a little frightened.

But he sat down beside her and laughed gently at the look on her face. "What are you expecting? I wonder. That I'll strip you and take you without preliminaries?"

Her eyes filmed. "I'm sorry...."

He touched her mouth with a hard finger. "Think about how it was on the beach, when I bent you back into the sand and kissed you, here." His fingers traveled down to her soft breasts. "And you threw back your head and moaned and begged me."

Her lips parted as she remembered vividly the sensations he'd aroused.

"That's how it's going to be now," he said, bending to her mouth. "Except that this time I'm not going to let you go."

His mouth opened hers with practiced ease, and his warm, callused hands were on her bare back, caressing it slowly and confidently, while all her inhibitions melted slowly away.

Seconds later the dress began to ease away from her body, and she felt his lips follow its downward movement. But she couldn't protest. The fires were burning again, and she moaned as his mouth covered her breasts, nipping at them with a tender pressure that was more arousing than frightening. His mouth followed as the dress merged with her tiny briefs and then was swept downward along with them. Shockingly, she felt his lips on her thighs, on the soft inner skin of her legs, and her body moved as the edge of his teeth followed the same path. Incredible, she thought through a fog of anguished desire, incredible that people could survive this kind of pleasure!

She wasn't even aware of what he was doing anymore; she was all sensation, all aching hunger. Her eyes were closed, her fists clenched beside her arched neck as his mouth searched her hips and her flat stomach. At the same time he was lazily divesting himself of his own clothing, making it so much a part of his seduction that she didn't even realize he'd done it until finally he slid alongside her and she felt him.

Her eyes flew open and went helplessly down the length of his body before she realized what she was doing. And then it was too late; she couldn't look away. He was glorious. Absolutely the most beautiful sight she'd ever seen, tanned all over without the slightest streak of white, as if he'd sunbathed in the nude all his life.

And meanwhile his hands touched her in a new intimate way. She started to draw away, but his mouth opened hers and his hands began a soft, tender rhythm, and soon she was weeping helplessly against his lips.

In seconds she was trembling and pleading with him. He moved, dragging his aching body into a sitting position against the headboard, his dark eyes glittering with frank desire. He lifted her over him and guided her, his body rigid with self-control, his face hard with it.

She gasped at the contact and her hands clenched on his shoulders as she found herself looking straight into his eyes.

"You do it," he told her huskily. "That way you can control the pain."

She started to argue, but she knew that it was becoming unbearable for him. She swallowed down her fear, closed her eyes, bit her lip and moved. She caught her breath and tried again.

"Help me, Eric," she begged, guiding his hands to her hips. "Please...oh!"

"It's bad, isn't it?" he ground out. "I'm sorry, I'm sorry...." His fingers contracted as his body began to fight his mind. The hunger was exploding in him. He began to tremble, his hands clenched. "Dani...!"

She opened her eyes at the new note in his voice and looked at him. The sight of his face took her mind off the pain. She watched him, fascinated. His eyes opened and found hers. Then his body seemed to take control away from his mind. His face changed, his breathing changed, the movements of his body intensified as she stared into his wild face. He arched and his face contorted, and all at once she realized what she was seeing and blushed wildly.

He was still for an instant, then he shuddered. His eyes opened slowly, looking into hers. His body still throbbed, his breathing unsteady and strained. His hands on her hips became caressing.

"I thought...you were dying," she whispered.

"I felt as if I were," he whispered back. His voice trembled, like his body, in the aftermath. His eyes searched her face. "You were watching me. Were you shocked?"

"Yes," she confessed, but she didn't look away.

"Was it bad?" he asked.

"Yes. Until I started watching you."

He brought her fully against him, still a part of him, and held her gently, with her face against his damp chest. "I think that was what pushed me over the edge," he murmured. "I saw you watching me and my head flew off."

"You looked as though you were being tortured to death."

"And you can't imagine pleasure so intense?" he chided her gently. He laughed, but it wasn't a taunting laugh. His hands caressed her back. "When I've rested for a few minutes I'm going to watch it happen to you."

"Will it?"

"Oh, yes. You just needed a few more seconds than I could give you. The second time," he added, easing her away from him, "always takes longer, for a man."

She looked into his eyes. "You're my lover now," she declared.

He looked down where they were still joined. Her eyes followed his and she blushed furiously.

"I'm still your lover," he told her. His hands pressed against her thighs, dragging her even closer, and all at once something happened that even her inexperienced body understood immediately.

He laughed softly. "Yes, you know what's going to happen now, don't you?" he growled. He shifted, easing her down onto the mattress as he loomed over her.

"Now," he said hotly, blazing with renewed passion. "Now watch what I'm going to do to you. Look!"

Her eyes dilated as she watched him. But the sensations were unexpected, and she cried out helplessly, her body lifting toward him as if it recognized its master.

"Shhhh," he hissed, smiling as her face began to contort. "Yes, you're going to feel it for me this time. I'm going to make you feel it, just as it happened to me. Yes, Dani, yes, yes...!"

She throbbed with a new rhythm. She moved and twisted and tried to throw him off, and tried to bring him back; she cried and pleaded and bit and whimpered and finally threw back her head and moaned so harshly that she sounded as if every bone in her body had snapped suddenly. And then it was all free-fall. Bonelessness. Purple oblivion.

When her eyes opened again she was exhausted. He sat on the bed beside her with a warm, damp cloth in his hands, bathing her gently.

"Is it always like that for men?" she asked, needing to know.

He shook his head. "It's never been like that for me with anyone. The second time was even more intense. I cried out."

Tears touched her eyes as she looked up at him. "Thank you."

"Oh, God, don't," he implored her, bending to kiss her. Once he kissed her he couldn't seem to stop. He put the cloth aside and took her into his arms, holding her, touching her face, brushing his lips over every soft, flushed inch of her face with a touch that was more healing than passionate.

She trembled in his arms, and they tightened, and she gloried in the delicious warmth of his skin against hers, the feel of her soft breasts being gently crushed by his hard-muscled chest.

"You cried out, too," he said at her ear. "Just as you felt it. I had to cover your mouth with mine so that no one would hear."

"Even in my dreams it never happened like that," she confessed.

"I'm glad it happened with me," he told her, lifting his head. "Thank you for waiting for me."

She smiled slowly. "I'm glad I waited."

"I didn't use anything," he said then. "Do you want to see a doctor tomorrow, or do you want me to take care of it until we get back to the States? A wife I can handle, but not a baby. Not yet."

"Then, could you...?" She hesitated. "I'd rather see my own doctor."

"Okay." He bent and brushed his mouth over hers.

"Do you want children eventually?" she asked because it was important.

He brushed the hair away from her eyes. "Perhaps," he said finally. "Someday."

"Too much, too soon?" she murmured dryly.

"Getting used to a wife is enough for now," he said. He let his eyes wander slowly over her. "You have a beautiful body."

"So have you."

He kissed her softly. "We'd better get some sleep. And, sadly enough, I do mean sleep." He sighed as he rose, cloth in hand. "I'm not prepared for anything else until we go into town. Unless...there are other ways if you really want..."

She blushed wildly and changed the subject. "Where are we getting married?"

"In a little chapel down the street." He grinned. "They're open at ten A.M. We'll be waiting on the doorstep."

"You aren't sorry?" she asked as he started into the bathroom.

He turned, his body open for her inspection, his face faintly smiling. He shook his head. "Are you?"

She shook her head, too. He laughed and went on into the bathroom. Minutes later she was curled up in his arms, both of them without a stitch on, the lights off and the sounds of the city at night purring in through the window.

"You can have one of my undershirts if you like," he said gently.

"I'd rather sleep like this, if it won't bother you," she murmured.

"I prefer it this way, too," he confessed. He drew her closer. "Breathing may be a little difficult, and I may die of a heart attack trying not to indulge myself a third time, but I prefer it like this. Good night, *lieveling*."

"Good night, Eric." She curled up against him with a trusting sigh and was surprised to find herself drifting off to sleep only seconds later.

Five

Dani was dreaming. She felt as if she were floating, drifting, her body bare and fulfilled. She stretched, smiling, and a voice brought her awake.

"Don't struggle, darling," a male voice chucked. "You'll make me drop you."

Her gray eyes flew open along with her mouth, and she realized that Dutch was carrying her into the bathroom, where a huge steaming bathtub waited.

"Don't you want a bath?" he murmured dryly.

"Oh, yes," she said sleepily. "I had planned on waking up before I got in the water." She curled into his chest, snuggled her face against his throat, and closed her eyes with a sigh. "But my pillow started moving."

He laughed, realizing with a start that he'd laughed more in the past two days than in the past ten years. He looked down at her creamy body, her full breasts pressed into the rippling muscle and feathery hair of his chest. She was vulnerable with him. Yet, he sensed that she was much like him in her independence, her wild spirit.

"Wake up or you'll drown," he said.

"I thought I already had, and gone to heaven," she replied, smiling against his throat. She wasn't even surprised to find herself with him. She seemed to have dreamed about him all night long.

"We have to get married," he said.

"Going to make an honest woman of me, hmmm?" she teased, peeking up at him.

But he didn't smile. "You're already an honest woman. The first I've ever known. Hold on."

He eased her down into the warm silky water and then climbed in beside her. They soaped each other lazily, enjoying the different textures of their bodies, exploring openly.

"I feel like a child playing doctor," he told her with a wicked glance.

"It's old hat to you, I suppose," she said, watching her hands move on his muscular chest, "but I've never touched a man like this. It's all very new to me just now."

He moved her hands down, watching the flush on her face and the panic in her yes. "All right," he said gently as she resisted. "You're still shy with me. I won't insist."

"Old maids have lots of hang-ups," she said quietly.

"I'll get rid of yours before the week's out," he promised. "Want some more soap?"

She let him lather her back. Something was niggling at the back of her mind, and she glanced at him worriedly as he rinsed her.

"What is it?" he asked gently.

"Something you said last night. About…about precautions."

"There's no problem," he said carelessly. "I'll stop by a drugstore. When we get back to the States, if you'd rather not risk the pill, there's some minor surgery a man can have—"

Her eyes were horrified. The drawn look on her face stopped him in mid-sentence.

"You don't ever want children, do you?" she asked, choking on the words.

He looked hunted. "Hell," he bit off. Why had she brought up the subject! He watched her scramble out of the tub and fumble a towel around herself.

"We aren't even married yet, and you're harping about a family," he burst out, rising to his feet, his handsome face hard with anger. "What the hell do we need kids for? They're a permanent tie. A bond."

"Isn't marriage?" she asked huskily.

"Of course," he grumbled, grabbing up a towel. "But not like kids."

"You never answered me," she said quietly. "You don't ever want them, do you?"

"No," he said flatly, tired of the pretense, hating the memories the discussion was bringing back. "Not ever."

She turned and walked back into the bedroom. She didn't know him at all. And the first thing she was going to do was cut her losses. She'd go back to her room and forget him. How could she expect to live all her life without a child? What kind of man was he?

Tears blinded her. She got as far as the bed and sat down, feeling empty and sick and alone. She'd dreamed of children. Since she was eighteen she'd haunted baby shops, quietly touching the little crocheted things and imagining her own baby in her arms. She had no one of her own, but a baby would be part of her. The tears rippled down her cheeks in silvery streams, and she closed her eyes.

The man at the bathroom door, watching her, saw them, and something painful exploded inside him. She was snaring him, he thought furiously. Swallowing him up whole with her unexpected vulnerabilities. With a muffled curse he threw the towel aside and went to the bed.

He caught her by the waist, lowering her back against the rumpled covers so quickly that she gasped.

"Eric!" she called uncertainly.

His mouth covered hers, but there was none of the violence she'd expected. His lips played with hers, so gentle that she barely felt them, while his hands removed the towel and whispered over her body until she trembled.

"Draw your legs up," he breathed. He helped her, positioning his body so that they were curled together, his knees beside her, his chest on hers, his hips against her hips and thighs.

She looked up, fascinated at the look in his dark eyes.

His big, warm hands cupped her face. "Open your mouth now," he whispered, bending, "and kiss me the way I taught you last night."

She obeyed him, liking the way her tongue tangled softly with his, liking the intimacy of this slow, tender kissing.

His knuckles brushed over her breasts, making their tips hard and sensitive, and when she gasped, his mouth took advantage of it to make the kiss even deeper. His hands searched over her, sliding under her hips to lift her to the slow descent of his body.

She felt his fingers contact on her thighs and caught her breath at their steely strength. And still he kissed her, whispery contacts that drained her of will, that made her weak. Her body trembled as he explored it with even more intimacy than the night before, each new touch intensifying her hunger for him.

He paused, hesitated, his lips touching hers. His eyes opened, holding hers, and his body lowered.

She caught her breath at the intensity of feeling she knew as he let her experience the very texture of his body with the slowness of his movement.

"Now," he said, closing his eyes, "we really make love for the first time."

She didn't understand at first. And then it began to make sense. He was so tender, so exquisitely gentle, that every movement seemed to stroke a nerve of pleasure. She clung to him, matching his tenderness, trying to give him back the beauty he was giving her. Her eyes fluttered closed and her fingers tangled in his cool blond hair, her body trembling under the expert movements of his. As the pleasure built slowly she began to writhe helplessly. And as fulfillment came closer, she wondered if she was going to survive it.

"Eric?" she whimpered against his mouth.

His own body was trembling, too. "*Lieveling,*" he said huskily. "*Mijn lieveling, mijn vrouw!*"

The hands holding her clenched, and he rocked with her, smooth, tender movements that were exquisitely soft. He whispered to her in Dutch, words that she couldn't understand, but they were breathlessly tender.

She kissed his tanned cheek, his mouth, his chin, and he lifted his head for an instant, his dark eyes glazed, his lips parted.

"Yes," he told her. "Yes, like that."

He closed his eyes and let her kiss him, savoring the softness of her mouth on his eyes, his cheeks, his straight nose, his lips.

She moved, trembling with need, letting him feel her body as she drew it with smooth sweetness to either side.

His eyes opened again, reading the intensity of hunger in hers.

"Yes," he said. "Yes, now it happens. Now..."

His voice didn't change, but his breathing did. He looked down at her, lengthening his movements, deepening them, so that although the tenderness remained, the urgency grew.

Something was happening to her that she didn't understand. Terrifying tension, hands buffeting her, a blazing tide of warmth that speared through her like tiny needles. Her mouth opened because she could no longer breathe. Her body began to shudder helplessly, tiny little shudders that matched the tenderness that was devouring her.

"I'm...afraid..." she managed, and her fingers clenched at his back as she felt her body beginning to contract.

"Hush," he said softly. His movements deepened, and still he watched. "Yes, feel it. Feel it now. There's nothing to be...afraid of, *lieveling*. No, don't turn away, let me see you...."

He turned her head back to him, and his face blurred. She thought he smiled, but she was all bursting fireworks, a flare lighting up the night sky. She felt gentle explosions all through her body, and for a moment her heart stopped, her breathing stopped. And then she cried, because it had been so beautiful, and so brief.

Even as the tears came, she felt his own body go rigid, heard the tender, surprised exclamation at her ear, and then her name....

He didn't move for a long time. Neither did she. She felt incapable of movement. What had happened surprised her. He'd said they wouldn't make love again until they got married, so why had he done it? And why that way? So tenderly, so gently, as if he cared about her.

Experimentally, her hands moved on the damp muscles of his shoulders.

He lifted his head and searched her eyes slowly. He touched her face with gentle fingers. "In my life there was never such a tender loving before," he said. "I didn't know that men and women were capable of it." He brushed away the tears. "I hurt you?" he asked.

"No." She swallowed. "It was. . .so beautiful," she faltered.

"Yes. For me, too." He drew away from her with exquisite slowness, watching her. He sighed heavily, and frowned. After a minute he turned back to the bathroom. "We'd better get dressed."

She got up, too, a little shaky and puzzled by his odd behavior. He'd meant to comfort her, she was certain of it. But the comfort had gotten out of hand. And the way he'd loved her. . .

As she dressed she wondered if she was doing the right thing, marrying a total stranger. Then he came out of the bathroom, wearing nothing except his slacks, his blond hair neatly combed, his face slowly curving into a smile. And she knew that she'd die to wear his ring, babies or no babies. She smiled back.

They were married in a small chapel, with people all around them who spoke little English. The minister beamed at them when it was over, inviting the new husband to kiss his bride.

Dutch bent and brushed his mouth softly against hers, smiling at his own folly. Well, it was done now. And it wouldn't be so bad, he told himself as he studied her radiant young face. She could wait for him at home, and they'd see each other whenever he was there. It might even be good that way. No routine to bore him. She could go on with her life, and there would be no ties. He frowned for a minute as he thought of what had happened this morning, then he shook off the instant fear of consequences. Surely to God, he hadn't made her pregnant. He'd just have to be careful from now on. No more lapses. The thought of a child terrified him. That would make a tie he couldn't break.

Dani saw that frown, and worried about it. She wondered why he'd really married her, when he seemed the kind of man who was self-sufficient and didn't need anyone else.

"You aren't sorry?" she asked finally when they were walking back to the hotel.

He stopped, lifted his blond head and smiled, a little puzzled. "What?"

"Sorry that you married me," she continued. She searched his eyes nervously. "You've been so quiet. I know I'm not much to look at, and we don't know each other at all. I...we can always get a divorce," she finished miserably.

"I'm quiet because I have a logistical problem to work out," he said then. "Not because I'm regretting that we got married. When you know me better, you'll learn that I never do things unless I want to. I can't be pushed or coerced." He reached out and curled her fingers into his. "I like being with you," he said, meeting her eyes. "Like this, and in bed. We're both old enough to want someone to be with."

"Yes," she confessed. Tears stung her eyes and she lowered her lids before he could read her thoughts. "I never thought it would happen to me," she added. "I thought I'd be alone all my life."

"So did I." He smoothed his fingers across the back of her hand. She had pretty hands, he mused. "Do you play anything?" he asked unexpectedly.

She laughed. "The piano. Badly."

"I like piano. I play a little, too." He slid his fingers in between hers, feeling oddly possessive as he saw the bright little gold band that encircled her ring finger. "A wedding ring suits you. Feel better now about what we did last night?" he asked with a slow smile, as if he understood her uneasiness about intimacy without marriage.

"I'm old-fashioned." She sighed miserably.

"You don't have to apologize for it, not to me." His eyes gleamed suddenly as he looked at her. Short brown hair, creamy, oval face, wide gray eyes. "I liked being the first."

There was a deep, possessive note in his voice that surprised her. She smiled slowly. Her fingers squeezed his, and she looked into his eyes for so long that she flushed.

"This morning," he said softly, holding her eyes, "was my first time. I didn't realize that I was capable of tenderness. I let go with you in a way I never could before with a woman. I trusted you."

Her face was bright red, but she didn't look away. "I...trusted you." She let her eyes fall to his hard mouth, remembering with a surge of desire how it felt on her body. "One of my friends got married two years ago. She said her husband shocked her speechless on her wedding night, and made fun of her...."

His fingers contracted. "I think it would kill something in you to have a man treat you so," he remarked.

Her eyes came up, stunned at the way he understood.

He nodded. "Yes. It's that way with me, too. I don't like ridicule."

Her expression said more than she wanted it to, and she knew that he could read the worshipful look in her eyes. But she didn't care. He was her whole world.

His breath caught at that look. It bothered him, and he let go of her hand. "Don't ever try to build a wall around me," he said unexpectedly, staring at her. "I'll stay with you only as long as the doors remain open."

"I knew that the first time I saw you," she said quietly. "No ties. No strings. I won't try to possess you."

He started walking again. He wondered what she was going to do when she knew the truth about him. He glanced up, searching her face quietly. She was so damned trusting. She probably thought he was in the army reserves or something. He almost laughed. Well, she'd just have to get used to it, he told himself, because he didn't know how to change.

After they'd changed their status at the hotel desk and switched everything to his room they went downstairs for lunch. Dani picked at her food, wondering at the change in Eric. Something was on his mind, but she didn't know him well enough to ask what it was. She glanced at him with a slow-dawning mischief in her eyes. Well, she couldn't dig it out of him, but she could help him forget it.

"Hey," she called.

He glanced up, cocking an eyebrow.

"I have this great idea for dessert," she murmured, making her first attempt at being a siren.

Both eyebrows went up. "You do?"

She dropped her eyes to his throat. "I could smear whipped cream all over myself..."

"Honey tastes better."

She blushed furiously, and he laughed. He leaned forward, moving his plate aside, and lifted her fingers to his mouth.

"Do you want me?" he asked bluntly, smiling at her averted face.

"Yes," she confessed.

"Then say so. You don't have to play games with me." He got up, helped her up, and paid the check. They were back in the hotel room before he spoke again.

He backed her up against the door and pinned her there with just the threat of his body. "You can have me anytime," he said quietly. "All you have to do is tell me. That's what marriage should be. Not some kind of power game."

Her eyes narrowed. "I don't understand."

He brushed the hair away from her face and curled it behind her ear. "Bargaining, with sex as the prize."

"I'd never do that," she said. She watched him, amazed that this handsome man was actually married to her. "You were worried about something. I wanted to...to give you peace."

He seemed to freeze. His lips parted on a hard breath. "I constantly misread you, don't I?" He touched her throat with the lightest touch of his fingers and lifted his eyes to hers. "Do you want me?"

"I'll want you on my deathbed," she said shakily.

He bent and kissed her softly, tenderly. "I'm more grateful than I can tell you, for such a sweet offer. But I don't think you can take me again today, not without considerable discomfort." He lifted his head. "Can you?"

She bit her lower lip. "Well..."

"Can you?"

She dropped her eyes to his chest. "Oh, shoot!" she mumbled. "No."

He laughed softly and drew her into his arms, rocking her slowly. "That's why I was so gentle this morning," he murmured into her ear, lying a little. He didn't want to admit that she'd been the victor in that tender battle.

"Oh." That was vaguely disappointing, she mused. She slid her arms around him with a sigh, delighting in his strength, the corded power of his warm hard body. "It isn't like this in books," she concluded. She smiled as her eyes closed. "Women always can, and they never have discomfort, and—"

"Life is very different," he said. He smoothed her hair. "We'll wait a day or so, until you recuperate. Then," he added, tilting her face up to his amused eyes, "I'll teach you some more subtle forms of sensual torture."

She laughed shyly. "Will you?"

He took a deep breath. "I've never known any-one like you," he said, the words reluctant. He drew her up on her tiptoes and kissed her very softly. "Feel what's happening already?"

"Yes," she answered him.

"We'd better cool it, if you don't mind. I hate cold showers."

She laughed. "You're terrific." She sighed.

"So are you. Get on a bathing suit and let's go swim."

She started into the bathroom, met his mocking eyes, and stuck out her chin. "You're my husband," she said aloud, to remind both of them.

"Yes, I was wondering if you might remember that." He chuckled.

She undressed and he watched, his eyes quiet and full of memories. When she started to pull on the bathing suit he moved in front of her and stayed her hands.

"Not yet," he said quietly.

She looked up, hungry for him, and watched as he studied her body and saw for himself just how much she wanted him.

"How is it, for a woman?" he asked suddenly, and sounded genuinely curious. "How do you feel when you want me like this?"

"It's frightening, a little," she told him. "I get shaky and weak and I can't quite control myself. I ache..."

"Does this...help the ache?" he asked as he bent to her breasts.

She moaned. It was impossible not to, when she felt the warm moistness of his lips eating her. She didn't have a mind left after the first two seconds. She was hardly aware that he was lifting her onto the bed.

He made a meal of her body, tasting, touching, looking at it, broad daylight streaming in the windows, while she gloried in the luxury of being married and enjoyed his pleasure in her.

"I love looking at your body," he said quietly, sitting beside her. His hands swept up and down, lingering on her soft curves. "I love touching it. Tasting it. I've never seen anything half so lovely."

"My husband," she whispered.

He looked up. "My wife."

Her body ached, and she knew he must feel the same longing she did. Her eyes asked a question, but he slowly shook his head.

"I won't do that to you," he said curtly. "Not ever will I take my pleasure and not give a thought to yours."

She ground her teeth together to stop the tears.

"And it isn't pity," he said, glaring at the look in her eyes. "I do nothing out of pity, least of all marry because of it, so you can stop looking at me that way. I want you and I'm getting irritable because I can't have you. So suppose you put on the bathing suit and I'll go have that damned cold shower and we'll swim."

He got up and she lay there, watching him as he discarded his clothing. Her lips parted as the last of the clothing came off, and she saw the urgency of his desire.

His body trembled as he looked at her, and she wanted to cry because of the torment she saw in his face.

"You said once...that there are...other ways," she ventured to ask. "Are there?"

His face hardened; his eyes glittered wildly. "Yes."

She held out her arms, her body throbbing, her blood running like a river in flood as she sensed that violence of his hunger. He hesitated only for a second before he came down beside her.

The days passed with miserable speed. They did everything together. They swam and talked, although always about general things rather than personal ones; they danced and sampled new delicacies at the dinner table. And at night he loved her. Sometimes in the early morning. Once on the bathroom floor because the strength of their desire hadn't left them time to get to bed. Sometimes he remembered precautions, but mostly he didn't, because his desire matched her own. She walked around in a sensual haze that blinded her to the future. But eventually, the day came when they had to look past Veracruz. It came suddenly, and too soon.

Six

The last day of their stay dawned unwelcomed, and Dani packed with a long face. She'd changed her plans so she could be with Dutch for his whole vacation, but at the end of the week he told her that he had a job waiting and couldn't spare any more time. She stared at him across the room as he got his own clothing together, wondering how dangerous his line of work was. A soldier, he'd said. Did that mean he was in the reserves? Probably, she told herself. That was why he wouldn't mind moving to Greenville.

She'd thought about that a lot, about picking up stakes and moving to Chicago. It wouldn't matter, although she'd miss Harriett and her friends from the bookstore. She'd have followed him anywhere. When she realized how little time they'd had together, she could hardly believe that so much had happened so quickly. It seemed like a lifetime ago that the taciturn blond giant had dropped down beside her on the airplane. And now he was her husband. Her husband, about whom she knew so little.

He seemed to feel her puzzled frown, and turned. Then he smiled at her. "Ready?" he asked as he picked up his duffel bag.

"Ready," she agreed. She drew her two bags up to where his were sitting by the door.

He glared at the smaller one and sighed. "You and your books." He chuckled softly down at her. "Well, at least now you know what they're all about, don't you?" he added.

She cleared her throat, reddening as she recalled the long, sweet nights. "Oh, yes, indeed I do, Mr. van Meer," she agreed fervently.

"No regrets, Dani?" he asked softly.

She shook her head. "Not if this were the last day of my life," she said. "And you?"

"I'm only sorry we met so late in life," he replied, searching her face. "I'm glad we found each other." He checked his watch. It was an expensive one, with dials and numbers that meant nothing to Dani. "We'd better rush or we'll miss our flight."

Dutch had made the reservation for the two of them and they had adjoining seats. She sat beside him with her heart in her throat, smiling at him with hopeless hero worship. He was so handsome. And hers. Harriett really wasn't going to believe this.

He glanced down at her, still amazed that he had a wife. J.D. and Gabby would be shocked, he thought. And Apollo and First Shirt, Semson and Drago and Laremos would never let him hear the end of it. Dutch, married. It was incredible, even to him. But it felt nice.

It was Gabby's influence, probably, he admitted to himself. He'd heard so much about her from J.D. even before he'd met her that some of his old prejudices against women had slackened. Not much, but a little. Gabby had trekked through a commando-infested jungle for J.D. and even risked her own life to save him from a bullet. He glanced again at his companion with narrowed dark eyes. Would she do that for him? Did she really possess the fiery spirit he sensed beneath her timid manners? And how was she going to react when she learned the truth about him? That hadn't bothered him for the past few days, but it bothered him now. A lot. His gaze went to the bag of romance novels tucked under her pretty feet. Fluff, he thought contemptuously, and a smile touched his firm mouth as he thought how nearly like fiction some of his exploits might seem to the woman beside him.

Dani saw him starting at her books and shifted uncomfortably in her seat. "Well, we can't all conquer the Amazon," she muttered.

His eyebrows shot up. "What?" He laughed.

"You were giving my books contemptuous glares," she said. "And if you're thinking it's all mushy nonsense, you might be surprised." She fished down and held up a book with a cover that featured a man armed with an automatic weapon. There was a jungle setting behind him and woman beside him.

Dutch blinked. Automatically, his hand reached for the book and he scowled as he flipped through it and glanced over the blurb on the back of the book jacket. The novel was about two photojournalists, trapped together in a Central American country during a revolution.

"Not what you expected?" she asked.

He lifted his eyes and studied her. "No."

She took the book from his hand and stuffed it back in her sack. "Most of us are armchair adventurers at heart, you know." She sighed. "Woman as well as men. You'd be amazed at how many of my customers fantasize about being caught up in a revolution somewhere."

His face hardened. He gave her a look that sent shivers through her.

"Dani, have you ever watched anyone die?" he asked bluntly.

She faltered, shocked by the icy challenge in his deep voice.

"No, of course not," she said.

"Then don't be too eager to stick your nose in some other country's military coups. It isn't pretty." He touched his pocket, reaching for a cigarette, then glanced up and noticed that the no-smoking sign was still lit as the plane climbed to gain more altitude. Then he also remembered that he'd chosen a seat in the no-smoking section to be near Dani, who didn't smoke. He said something rough under his breath.

"Have you?" she asked unexpectedly. "Stuck your nose in somebody's military coups?" she added when he lifted an eyebrow.

"That would hardly concern you," he said, softening the words with a smile.

He wasn't exactly rude, but she turned quickly back to the window in silence. She felt uneasy, and tried to banish the feeling. He was her husband now. She'd have to learn not to ruffle him. She leaned back, closed her eyes and convinced herself that she was worrying needlessly. Surely there were no dark secrets in his past.

Someone in the seat ahead of them rang for the stewardess, and Dani closed her eyes, thinking what a long flight this was going to be. They'd planned to stop over in Greenville and then decide who would move and who wouldn't. He wanted to see where she lived, he'd said, to meet her friend Harriett and see the little bookshop she owned. She'd been flattered by his interest.

She had just closed her eyes when she heard a loud gasp and then a cry from nearby. Her eyes opened to see the stewardess being held roughly by a man in brown slacks and an open-necked white shirt. He had a foreign look, and his eyes were glazed with violence. At the stewardess's neck he was holding a hypodermic syringe. Another man who had been sitting with him got calmly to his feet, walked around the man with the syringe and went into the cockpit.

There was a loud yell and the copilot appeared, took one look at what was happening and seemed to go white.

"Yes, he's telling the truth, as near as I can tell," the copilot called into the cockpit.

There was a buzz of conversation that was unintelligible, then the captain's voice came over the loudspeaker and Dutch stiffened, his dark gaze going slowly over the man with the syringe.

"Ladies and gentlemen, this is Captain Hall." The deep voice was deceptively calm. "The plane is being diverted to Cuba. Please keep calm, remain in your seats and do exactly as you're told. Thank you."

The unarmed man came out of the cockpit, twitching his thick mustache, and fumbled around with the intercom until he figured it out.

"We wish no one to be harmed," he said. "The syringe my friend is holding to the neck of this lovely young lady is filled with hydrochloric acid." Shocked murmurs went through the crowd, especially when the shorter, bald man took the syringe to one side and deliberately let one drop fall on the fabric of the seat. It smoldered and gave a vivid impression of the impact it would have on the stewardess's neck. "So for the young lady's sake, please keep calm," he continued. "We will harm you only if you make it necessary."

He hung up the intercom and went back into the cockpit. The man with the syringe tugged the petite blond stewardess along with him, ignoring the passengers. Apparently, he thought the threat of the syringe was enough to prevent any interference.

And it seemed he was right. The other passengers murmured uneasily among themselves.

"Professionals," Dutch said quietly. "They must want to get out of the country pretty badly."

Dani eyed him uncomfortably. "Who are they, do you think?"

"No idea," he said.

"They wouldn't really use that acid on her?" she asked, her voice soft with astonishment.

He turned and looked down at her, into gray eyes more innocent than any he'd ever seen. He frowned. "My God, of course they'd use it!"

Her oval face paled. She looked past him to where one of the men was barely visible, his arm still around the stewardess.

"Can't the captain do something?" she said then.

"Sure." He leaned back in his seat and closed his eyes, clasping his lean, tough hands over his stomach. "He can do exactly what they tell him until they get off the plane. All they want is a free ride. Once they've had it, they'll leave."

She gnawed on her lower lip. "Aren't you worried?" she asked.

"They aren't holding the syringe to my neck."

His indifference shocked her. She was terrified for the stewardess. Horrified, she forced her eyes back to her lap. For God's sake, what kind of man had she married?

He closed his eyes again, ignoring her contemptuous stare. He regretted the need to shock her, but he needed time to think, and he couldn't do it if she was talking. Now he had sufficient quiet to put together a plan. They wouldn't hurt the girl if their demands were met. But glitches sometimes happened. In case one developed, he had to think of a way out. There were two men, but only one was armed. And obviously, they hadn't been able to get anything metallic through the sensors. That was good. They might have a plastic knife or two between them, or a pocket knife like the one Dutch was carrying—a knife that had special uses. His was balanced and excellent for throwing. And he had few equals with a knife. He smiled.

Dani glanced at Dutch with mingled hurt and curiosity and rage. He was asleep, for heaven's sake! In the middle of a hijacking, he was asleep! She sighed angrily. Well, what did she expect him to do? Leap up from the seat like one of the heroes in the books she read and deliver them all from the terrorists? Fat chance!

A hijacking. She sighed, nervously fingering her purse. She wondered how the poor stewardess felt.

The woman was doing her best to stay calm, but it couldn't have been easy. Knowing what was in that syringe, and how quickly it would work if she were injected with it. . .Dani shuddered at just the thought. In her innocence she'd never believed that there were such fiendish people sharing the world with her.

Dutch opened one eye and closed it again. Dani gave him an exasperated look and clasped her hands to still their trembling. The taller of the hijackers had something in his hand that looked suspiciously like a grenade, and as the plane grew closer to Cuba, he began to pace nervously.

The shorter hijacker, the bald one who was holding the stewardess prisoner, moved into view. He forced the stewardess into the front seat, which was just one ahead of Dutch and Dani, and sat beside her, with the syringe still at her throat.

He was tiring, Dutch mused. And the other one was getting a little panicky. His dark eyes narrowed thoughtfully. He'd bet his life that the grenade was plastic. How else could they have cleared airport security? One of the magazines on covert operations ran advertisements for the fakes—they were dirt cheap and, at a distance, realistic enough to fool a civilian. Which Dutch wasn't.

He'd wait until the plane landed in Cuba. If they were granted asylum, fine. If not, he was going to put a monkey wrench into their act. He owed it to Dani, sitting so quiet and disillusioned beside him.

You know the thrill of escaping to a world of PASSION...SENSUALITY ...DESIRE...SEDUCTION... and LOVE FULFILLED...

Escape again...with 4 FREE novels and

Get more great Silhouette Desire novels —for a 15-day FREE examination— delivered to your door every month!

*S*ilhouette Desire offers you real-life drama 'and romance of successful women in charge of their lives and their careers, women who face the challenges of today's world to make their dreams come true. They are not for everyone, they're for women who want a sensual, provocative reading experience.

These are modern love stories that begin where other romances leave off. They take you *beyond* the others and into a world of love fulfilled and passions realized. You'll share precious, private moments and secret dreams...experience every whispered word of love, every ardent touch, every passionate heartbeat. And now you can enter the unforgettable world of Silhouette Desire romances each and every month.

FREE BOOKS

You can start today by taking advantage of this special offer— 4 new Silhouette Desire romances (a $9.00 Value) *absolutely FREE,* along with a Mystery Gift and FREE Cameo Tote Bag. Just fill out and mail the attached postage-paid order card.

AT-HOME PREVIEWS, FREE DELIVERY

After you receive your 4 free books, Tote Bag and Mystery Gift, every month you'll have the chance to preview 6 more Silhouette Desire romances *—as soon as they are published.* When you decide to keep them, you'll pay just $11.70, (a $13.50 Value), *with no additional charges of any kind and no risk!* You can cancel your subscription at any time just by dropping us a note. In any case, the first 4 books, Tote Bag and Mystery Gift are yours to keep.

EXTRA BONUS

When you take advantage of this offer, we'll also send you the Silhouette Books Newsletter free with every shipment. Every informative issue features news on upcoming titles, interviews with your favorite authors, and even their favorite recipes.

Get a Free Tote Bag and Mystery Gift, too!

EVERY BOOK YOU RECEIVE WILL BE A BRAND-NEW FULL-LENGTH NOVEL!

Escape with 4 Silhouette Desire novels and get a Tote Bag and Mystery Gift, too!

Silhouette Desire®

Silhouette Books, 120 Brighton Rd., P.O. Box 5084, Clifton, NJ 07015-9956

Yes, please send me FREE and without obligation, 4 new Silhouette Desire novels along with my Tote Bag and Mystery Gift. Unless you hear from me after I receive my 4 FREE books, please send me 6 new Silhouette Desire novels for a free 15-day examination each month as soon as they are published. I under- stand that you will bill me a total of just **$11.70** (a $13.50 Value), with no additional charges of any kind. There is no minimum number of books that I must buy, and I can cancel at any time. The first 4 books, Tote Bag and Mystery Gift are mine to keep, even if I never take a single additional book.

NAME _____

(please print)

ADDRESS _____

CITY _____ STATE _____ ZIP _____

She still believed in heroes, although God alone knew what she thought of him right now.

When the plane landed in Havana the shorter man stayed beside the stewardess while the taller one went into the cockpit. He stayed there only a few minutes, and then burst out the small doorway with wild eyes, cursing violently.

"What is it? What is it!" the smaller man demanded.

"They will not let us disembark! They will not give us asylum!" the taller man cried. He looked around wildly, clasping the forgotten grenade in his hands and ignoring the horrified looks and cries of the passengers. "What shall we do? They will give us fuel but not asylum. What shall we do? We cannot go back to Mexico!"

"*Cuidado!*" the older man cautioned sharply. "We will go to Miami. Then we will seek asylum from our backers overseas," he said. "Tell them to fly to Miami."

Now, that was interesting, Dutch thought as he watched the taller man hesitate and then go back into the cockpit. He had a hunch that the gentlemen with the stage props were Central American natives. But obviously they had no wish to be connected with any of the Central American countries. And that talk of comrades overseas sounded very familiar. As almost everyone knew, there were foreign interests at work all over Central America.

The taller man was back in a minute. "They are turning toward Miami," he told his companion.

"*¡Bueno!*" The short man sounded relieved. "Come."

He forced the stewardess to her feet and dragged her along with him as he urged the tall man toward the cockpit. "We will explain the demands the pilot is to present to the American authorities," the short one murmured.

Dutch's eyes opened. "How much courage do you have, Mrs. van Meer?" he asked Dani without turning his head. His voice was low enough that only she could hear it.

She tensed. What in the world did he mean? "I'm no coward," she managed.

"What I have in mind could get you killed."

Her heart leaped. "The stewardess!"

He looked down at her. His eyes were dark and quiet and his face was like so much granite. "That will depend on you. When we approach that airport I want you to distract the man with the syringe. Just distract him. Force him to move that syringe for just a fraction of a second."

"Why do anything?" she asked softly. "You said that they'd leave—"

"Because they're desperate now," he said quietly. "And I have no doubt whatsoever that one of their demands is going to be for automatic weapons. Once they have those, we've lost any chance of escape."

"The authorities won't give them weapons," she said.

"Once they've used that acid on a couple of people they will," he said.

She shuddered again. She could taste her own fear, but Dutch seemed oddly confident. He also seemed to know what he was doing. She looked up into his eyes with returning faith. No, she told herself, she'd been reading him wrong. All that time he'd been quiet, he'd been thinking. And now she trusted him instinctively.

"You could be killed," he repeated, hating the words even as he said them. How could he put her in danger? But how could he not take the chance? "There's a risk; I won't minimize it."

She sighed. "Nobody would miss me, except maybe you and Harriett," she said dryly.

He felt odd. She didn't say it in a self-pitying way. It was just a simple statement of fact. Nobody gave a damn. He knew how that felt himself, because outside the group nobody cared about him, either. Except for Dani. And he cared about her, too. He was suddenly vulnerable because of her, he realized.

She looked up at him with wide gray eyes that had seen too little living to be closed forever.

"There's a chance I could manage it alone," he began slowly.

"I'm not afraid," she said. "Well, that is, I am afraid, but I'll do whatever you tell me to."

So Gabby wasn't a freak after all, he told himself, gratified to find Dani so much like his best friend's wife. This little dove had teeth, just as he'd suspected.

He smiled faintly. "Okay, tiger. Here's what I want you to do...."

She went over it again and again in her mind in the minutes that followed. She chewed her lower lip until it was sore, and then chewed it some more. She had to get it right the first time. The poor stewardess wouldn't have a second chance. If they failed—and she still didn't realize how Dutch was going to get to that man in time—the stewardess would die.

She agonized over it until the captain announced that the plane was on its approach to Miami. He cautioned the passengers to stay calm and not panic, and to stay in their seats once the plane was on the ground. He sounded as strained as Dani felt. That hand grenade was the most terrifying part of all, and she wondered how Dutch was going to prevent the second man from throwing it.

The plane circled the airport and went down, landing roughly this time, bumping around as it went toward the terminal. Dani got her first glimpse of Miami and thought ironically that she sure was getting to see a lot of the world!

As soon as the plane came to a halt, Dutch touched her arm and looked down at her. Dani closed her eyes on a brief prayer.

The man with the syringe had just moved back into the cabin. He looked taut and nervous as well. The stewardess looked as though she'd given up all hope of living and had resigned herself to the horror of the acid. Her eyes were blank.

"Uh, señor...?" Dani called, getting halfway out of her seat.

The short man jumped at the sound of her voice and his arm tightened around the stewardess. "What you want?" he growled.

"I...oh, please..." Dani clutched the back of the seat and her gray eyes widened as she fought to make the words come out. "I have to go...to the rest room, please..."

The short man cursed. He called something in another language to the man in the cockpit, who looked out, angrily.

"I have to!" Dani pleaded, looking and sounding convincing.

The tall man muttered something and the short one laughed curtly. "All right," he said after a minute, during which Dani aged five years. "Come on, then."

She slipped over Dutch, and while she was moving, his hand went slowly to his inside jacket pocket.

Dani moved into the aisle and started carefully toward the rest room on the other side of the man with the syringe. Two more steps, she told herself. Her heart pounded, and she kept her eyes cast downward in case the man saw the terror in them and reacted too quickly. One more step. Please don't fail me, she said silently to Dutch. This is insane, I'm only twenty-six, I don't want to die, I've only just gotten married!

One more step. And she stopped and swayed, putting a hand to her temple. "I'm so sick!" And it was almost the truth. She deliberately let herself fall toward him.

It was enough. It was enough. He instinctively moved to catch her, and at that instant Dutch threw the knife. The syringe went to the floor as the hijacker caught his middle. Dutch was out of his seat in a heartbeat. It was 'Nam all over again. Angola. Rhodesia. He ignored Dani, who was watching with incredulous eyes, tore the stewardess out of the hijacker's helpless grasp, threw her into a seat and kicked the hypodermic out of the way. He was through the cockpit door seconds after he'd thrown the knife, ignoring the groaning bald man on the floor as he went for the taller man.

"I will throw it, señor!" the man threatened, and grasped the firing pin of the grenade.

"Go ahead," Dutch said, and kept going. With two movements of his hands, so quick that the pilot didn't even see them, the hijacker went down with the grenade in his hand.

"He's pulled the pin!" the young copilot yelled, and there was pandemonium in the airplane.

"For God's sake," Dutch growled, retrieving it, "what are you afraid of, flying bits of plastic?"

And he tossed the cheap imitation into the pilot's lap.

The copilot started to dive for it, but the pilot, a man in his late forties, just laughed. He turned toward Dutch and grinned.

"I should have realized why he was so nervous."

The copilot was still gaping. "It's a fake!"

"Keep it for a souvenir." The pilot sighed, tossing it to his colleague. "How's Lainie?"

"If you mean the stewardess, she's okay," Dutch said. "But his buddy isn't. You'd better get a doctor out here."

"Right away. Hey. Thanks," the pilot said with a quiet smile.

Dutch shrugged. "Pure self-interest," he said. "He was holding up my coffee."

"I'll buy you a cup when we get out of here," the captain offered.

Dutch grinned. "Take you up on that."

He left the cockpit. "It wasn't a live grenade," he called, the authority in his voice pacifying the nervous passengers. "It's all over, just sit quietly."

Dani was sitting on the floor, staring horrified at the groaning man with the knife in his stomach while she tried to deal with what was happening. She looked up at the stranger she'd married without even recognizing him. Who was he?

Dutch was sorry she'd had to see it, but there was no other way to do it. He bent and caught her by the arms and pulled her up gently.

"He'll be okay," he said. "No sweat. Let's get off this thing." He pulled her toward the door. Two other flight attendants came rushing from the back of the plane, embracing the stewardess, apologizing for not being able to help.

"It's okay," the little blond said shakily. "I'm fine."

She turned to Dutch, all blue eyes and gratitude. "Thank you. Thank you both!"

"All in a day's work," Dutch said carelessly. "How about getting this door open? That man needs a medic."

The groaning man got their attention. One of the flight attendants bent over him, and the co-pilot was just frog-marching the second terrorist, whose hands were belted together behind him, into the service compartment.

"Wait and I'll show you to the office," the captain called to Dutch. "We'll need to speak to the police, I'm sure."

"Okay," Dutch told him. He propelled Dani, who was still half shocked, down the stairs with him, out into the darkness. "Oh," he said, turning and addressing the male flight attendant, "would you please get the lady's books and purse out of seat 7B and bring them to the office?"

"Be glad to, sir," came the reply.

Dani was still shocked, but her mind registered what he'd just said. In the middle of all the furor he'd remembered her blessed books. She looked up at him uncomprehendingly, her eyes wide and frightened and uncertain and still bearing traces of sick terror.

"I had to," he said quietly as he recognized the look. "I couldn't have reached him in time."

"Yes, I—I realize that. I've just never seen anybody...like that."

"You were superb," he said. "I can think of only one other woman who would have kept her head so well."

She wondered whom he meant, but there were more immediate questions. "What...what you did," she faltered as they waited for the captain. "You said you were a soldier."

He turned her gently and held her in front of him, holding her wary gaze. "I am. But not the kind you're thinking of. I make my living as a professional soldier. I hire out to the highest bidder," he told her bluntly, without pulling his punches, and watched the horror that filled her face. He hadn't realized how devastated she was going to be, or how he might feel when he saw the horror in her innocent face. Her reaction surprised him. It irritated him. What had she expected, for God's sake, a clerk?

"A mercenary," she said in a choked tone.

"Yes," he replied, his whole stance challenging.

But she didn't say anything more. She couldn't. Her dreams were lying around her feet, and she hurt all the way to her soul. This news was much more devastating than what she'd seen on the plane. She didn't lift her eyes again; she didn't speak. Seconds later the pilot, copilot and stewardess who'd been held prisoner joined them, and they went to the airport office. Dani walked apart from Dutch, not touching him. He noticed that, and his face was grim when they got into the building.

Minutes later they were sitting in a small office, going over and over what had happened for the airport security people and three men who looked very much like federal officers. It didn't take long, and they were told that they'd have to appear in court, but Dani hardly heard any of it. She was trying to deal with the realization that she was married to a professional mercenary soldier. And she didn't know what to do.

Her eyes studied him as he spoke to the other men. He didn't look like one. But the air of authority that had puzzled her, his confidence, the way he seemed to take command of things—yes, it made sense now. She even knew when it had happened, back when that woman had made a fool of him. That was the beginning. And now he had a life-style he liked, and a biddable little wife who'd be waiting back at home while he went around the world looking for trouble.

She lifted the cup of coffee they'd brought her and sipped it quietly. No, sir, she thought, her eyes narrowing. No, sir, she wasn't going to be his doormat. She cared for him, but there had to be more to a relationship than sex. And if that was all he wanted from her, he could go away.

A cold sickness washed over her as she realized how much a part of her life he'd become. So quickly, he'd absorbed her. All she had to do was look at him and she ached to hold him, to be loved by that warm, powerful body. She knew so much about him, things she blushed even remembering. But none of it was real. She couldn't sit alone at home while he went out and risked his life. My God, she thought, no wonder he didn't want children! How could he have kids in his line of work? They'd never even see their father! As for Dani, how could she live with worry eating at her like an acid? Every time he left she'd be wondering if she'd ever see him again. She'd wonder, and not know, and eventually the not-knowing would kill her soul. No, she thought miserably. Better to have a sweet memory than a living nightmare. He'd have to divorce her. She knew already that he wouldn't give up his way of life. And she couldn't stay married to him under the circumstances. So there was nothing left. A dream, ending too soon.

After the meeting was over they walked quietly outside the terminal. The captain followed them, along with the male flight attendant who brought Dani's purse and her sack of books.

"What now?" she asked helplessly.

"The airline will pay for hotel rooms," the captain said with a kind smile. "Tomorrow we'll fly you to Greenville."

Dutch looked hunted as he glanced over the captain's shoulder. "The press corps has taken up residence," he growled.

"No stomach for stardom?" the captain grinned.

"None whatsoever," came the taut reply. "Dani and I are catching the next flight out of here tonight," he added flatly. "I'm afraid that the international wire services will have a field day."

"Probably so," the captain agreed. "It seems our erstwhile hijackers have some interesting ties to a certain Central American dictator and a few communist strings as well." He sighed. "They'd have wanted weapons once we landed," he said, glancing at Dutch.

"Yes. And they'd have gotten them," the blond man said. He lit a cigarette.

"Used that knife very often?" the captain asked quietly.

Dutch nodded. "Far too often, in years past."

"Would you mind telling me what occupation you're in?" he was asked.

Dutch eyed him quietly. "Care to make an educated guess?"

"Covert operations."

He nodded, noticing Dani's hollow-eyed stare. He looked down at her with unreadable eyes. "I'm a professional mercenary. My specialty is logistics, but I'm handy with small arms as well, and I have something of a reputation with that knife. I made it myself." He glanced at the captain. "When the surgeons get it removed, I'd like to have it back."

The captain nodded. "I'll have it gold-plated, if you like. You saved us one hell of a mess. Any time you need help, just let me know."

"That isn't likely, but thank you."

The captain walked away and Dutch smoked his cigarette quietly while the press converged on the pilot once he was alone.

"Is that why you wanted to avoid the press?" Dani asked hesitantly. He frightened her. Despite the fact that she'd read *The Dogs of War* twice and seen the film three times, she could hardly believe what she was hearing. It was like watching a movie. All of it. The hijacking, the way he'd handled the hijackers, the matter-of-fact way he'd dealt with all of it. Her eyes were glued to his face while she turned it all around in her mind. She was married to a soldier of fortune. Now what was she going to do?

He saw that look in her eyes and could have cursed. Fate was giving him a hard time.

"I don't like publicity," he said. "My private life is sacred."

"And where do I fit into your life?" she asked quietly. It was too soon to ask that, but things needed to be said now.

"You're my wife," he said simply.

"Why did you marry me?" she asked.

He looked hunted. His eyes narrowed, his jaw clenched. He took a deep puff of his cigarette before he replied. "I wanted you."

So that was all, she thought. It didn't hurt, although she was sure it was going to, when the numbness wore off. She was still in a state of shock. She had risked her life, seen a man wounded in front of her eyes, learned that her husband was a mercenary....

He was watching her face, and he felt a violence of emotion that made him dizzy. She was under his skin. In his very soul. How did he get her out?

"Yes, I thought so," she said too casually. She searched the face her hands had touched so lovingly. "And what did you expect that our married life would be like? That I'd sit home and wait while you went away and came home shot to pieces year after year?"

He felt shocked. Taken by surprise. He stared at her intently. "I thought...we'd each have our own lives. That we could enjoy each other. Belong to each other."

She shook her head. "No. I'm sorry. I couldn't live that way. You'd better divorce me."

It was almost comical. His spinster wife of a week was showing him the door. Him! Women had chased him for years. They'd practically hung out windows trying to snare him because of his very elusiveness. And this plain little frumpy bookseller was showing him the door!

"You needn't look so shocked," she told him. "I'm only saving myself a little heartache, that's all. I can't live with the knowledge that your life is constantly in danger. I'd be destroyed."

"I'm not suicidal, for God's sake," he began.

"You're not superhuman, either," she reminded him. "There are scars on you. I didn't realize what they were at the time, but now I know. And one day you'll stop a bullet. I don't want to be sitting alone waiting for the phone to ring. I'm strong. But I'm not that strong. I care too much."

It amazed him that he felt those last four words to the soles of his feet. She cared about him. Of course she did; it was written all over her, in the soft gray eyes that had worshipped him when he loved her, in the hands that had adored him. It was infatuation or hero worship, he knew, but it had been flattering. Now it meant something more to him. Now it mattered that she was turning him away.

"We'll talk when we get to Greenville," he said firmly.

"You can talk all you like," she said, walking away from him. "I've had my say."

"You little frump!" he burst out, infuriated.

"Look who's calling whom a frump!" she threw back, whirling, all big angry gray eyes behind her glasses and flying hair and flushed cheeks. "Who do you think you are, big, bad soldier. God's gift?"

He wanted to strangle her, but he laughed instead.

"And don't laugh at me," she fumed. "It was all a line, wasn't it? You told me I was beautiful to you, but I was just a pickup, something to play with between wars!"

"At first," he agreed. He finished his cigarette and ground it out under his shoe. "But not now."

"That's right, now I'm a liability," she told him. "I'm a holiday interlude that's over."

He shook his blond head. She got prettier by the day, he mused, watching her. He'd called her a frump only because he was so angry. He smiled slowly. "You aren't over, pretty girl."

"I'm a frump!" she yelled at him.

A passing flight attendant grinned at her. "Not quite," he murmured, and winked.

Dani picked up her bag of books and started walking toward the terminal.

"Where are you going?" Dutch asked.

"Back home," she told him. "I've got a bookstore to run."

"Stop."

She did, but she kept her back to him. "Well?"

He hesitated. It was uncharacteristic. He didn't know what to do next. If he pushed her, he could lose her. But he couldn't let go, either. She'd become important to him. He didn't want to think about never seeing her again.

"Thank about it for a while," he said finally. "For a few weeks, until I get back."

"Back?" She turned, not caring if he saw her pain. Tears bit at her eyelids and she felt sick all over.

Oh, God, it hurt to see her like this! He glared toward the horizon, jamming his hands into his pockets. He'd never seen that expression on a woman's face in his life. He'd come to the brink of death with cool disdain more times than he cared to remember, and now the look on a woman's face terrified him.

She fought to get herself under control. She took a slow, deep breath. "I won't change my mind," she said, sure now that it would be suicide to stay with him.

"All the same, I'll be in touch."

"Suit yourself."

He met her eyes, searching them. "I'm already committed to this job. I can't back out." It was the first time in years that he'd explained himself, he realized.

"I don't want to know," she said firmly. "You have your life, and I have mine. If you'd told me in the very beginning, I wouldn't have come near you."

"I think I knew that," he said softly. He sketched her with his eyes, memorizing her. "Take care of yourself."

"I always have." She let her eyes love him one last time. She ached already at their parting. It would be like losing a limb. "You take care of yourself, too."

"Yes."

She stared at her wedding ring, and he saw the thought in her eyes.

"Leave it on," he said gently. "I—would like to think that you were wearing my ring."

The tears burst from her eyes. She didn't even look at him again, she turned and broke into a run, suitcases and all, crying so hard that she could hardly see where she was going. Behind her he stood quietly on the apron, alone, watching until she was out of sight.

Seven

Nothing was the same. The first day she was home Dani went into the bookstore the same as always, but her life was changed. Harriett Gaynor, her small, plump friend, gave her odd looks, and Dani was almost certain that Harriett didn't believe a word of the story her employer told her about the Mexican holiday. Then the next day the papers hit the stands.

"It's true!" Harriett burst out, small and dark-eyed, her black hair in tight curls around her elfin face. "It's all here in the paper, about the hijacking, look!"

Dani grimaced as she looked down at the newspaper Harriett had spread over the counter. There was a picture of the pilot, and a blurred one of the uninjured hijacker being carried off the plane. There wasn't a picture of Dutch, but she hadn't expected to see one. He seemed quite good at dodging the press.

"Here's something about the man who overpowered the hijacker..." Harriett frowned and read, catching her breath at the vivid account. She looked up at Dani. "You did that?"

"He said they would have asked for automatic weapons once we were in Miami," Dani said quietly.

Harriett put the paper down. "A professional mercenary." She stared at her best friend. "I don't believe it. Didn't you ask what he did before you married him?"

"If you saw him, you wouldn't be surprised that I didn't," Dani told her. She turned away. She didn't want to talk about Dutch. She wanted to forget. Even now, he was on his way to another conflict....

"No man is that good-looking," Harriett said. "Not even Dane." Dane, a pleasant man, wasn't half the scrapper his pint-sized wife was. "By the way, Mrs. Jones called to thank you for her autographed books."

"She's very welcome. It was nice, getting to meet some of the authors at the autographing." She checked the change in the cash register as they started to open the shop.

"Where is he now?" Harriett asked suddenly.

"Getting a good lawyer, I hope," Dani said, laughing even though it hurt to say it. "We're setting a new record for short marriages. One week."

"You might work it out," came the quiet reply.

Dani wouldn't look at her friend. "He makes his living risking his life, Harrie," she said. "I can't spend mine worrying about him. I'd rather get out while I still can."

"I suppose you know your own mind," Harriett said, shrugging. "But when you decide to go adventuring, you sure go whole hog, don't you? Marrying strangers, overpowering hijackers..."

She went away muttering, and Dani smiled at her retreating back. Yes, she'd had an adventure all right. But now it was over, and she'd better tuck her bittersweet memories away in a trunk and get on with her life. The first step was to put Dutch out of her mind forever. The second was to stop reading the newspaper. From now on, every time she learned about a small foreign war, she'd see him.

Of course, it wasn't that easy. In the weeks that followed, everything conspired to remind her of him. Especially Harriett, who became heartily suspicious when Dani began losing her breakfast.

"It's the curse of Montezuma," Dani said shortly, glaring at her friend from a pasty face as she came out of the bathroom with a wet paper towel at her mouth.

"It's the curse of the flying Dutchman," came the dry reply.

Dani laughed in spite of herself, but it was brief. "I am not pregnant."

"I had a miscarriage," Harriett said quietly. "But I've never forgotten how it felt, or how I looked. You're white as a sheet, you tire so easily it isn't funny, and your stomach stays upset no matter what you do."

It was the same thing Dani had been dreading, hoping, terrified to admit. But she'd arrived at the same conclusion Harriett had. She sat down on the stool behind the counter with a weary sigh.

"You crazy child, didn't you even think about contraceptives?" Harriett moaned, hugging her.

Harriett, only four years her senior, sometimes seemed twice that. Dani let the tears come. She wept so easily these days. Last night a story on the news about guerrilla action in Africa had set her off when she spotted a blond head among some troops. Now, Harriett's concern was doing it, too.

"I'm pregnant," Dani whispered shakily.

"Yes, I know."

"Oh, Harrie, I'm scared stiff," she said, clutching the older woman. "I don't know anything about babies."

"There, there, Miss Scarlett, I doesn't know anything about birthin' babies my own self, but we'll muddle through somehow." She drew away, smiling with a genuine affection. "I'll take care of you." She searched Dani's eyes. "Do you want to have it?"

Dani shuddered. "I saw a film once, about how babies develop." She put her hand slowly, tenderly, to her flat abdomen. "They showed what happened when a pregnancy is terminated." She looked up. "I cried for hours."

"Sometimes it's for the best," Harriett said gently.

"In some circumstances," she agreed. "But I'll never see it as a casual answer to contraception. And as for me," she said shifting restlessly, "—I. . .want his baby." She clasped her arms around herself with a tiny smile. "I wonder if he'll be blond?" she mused.

"He may be a she," came the dry reply.

"That's all right. I like little girls." She sighed dreamily. "Isn't it amazing? Having a tiny life inside you, feeling it grow?"

"Yes," Harriett said wistfully. "It was the happiest time of my life."

Dani looked up and smiled. "You can share mine."

Harriett, tougher than nails, grew teary-eyed. She turned quickly away before Dani could see that vulnerability. "Of course I can. Right now you need to get to a doctor and see how far along you are."

"I already know," Dani said, remembering the morning in Dutch's room, the exquisite tenderness of that brief loving. "I know."

"You'll need vitamins," Harriett continued. "And a proper diet."

"And baby clothes and a baby bed..." Dani was dreaming again.

"Not until after the seventh month," Harriett said firmly. "You have to be realistic, too. Sometimes it happens, sometimes it doesn't. But it helps not to get too involved too soon."

"Spoilsport!" Dani burst out, half-irritated.

"The doctor will tell you the same thing," Harriett said. "Dani, I bought baby furniture when I was a month along. I miscarried at four months, and had all those bright new things to dispose of. Don't do it."

Dani immediately felt repentant. She hugged Harriett warmly. "Thank you for being my friend. For caring about me."

"Someone has to." She glowered up at Dani. "Are you going to tell him?"

"How?" Dani asked. "I don't even know his address."

"My God, she's married to a man and she doesn't know where he lives."

Dani laughed at the expression on Harriett's face. "Well, we didn't spend much time talking."

Harriett started at the young woman's belly. "So I noticed."

"Stop that!" Dani sighed wearily. "Besides, he said he never wanted children. He'd go right through the roof if he knew. It's just as well that the divorce go through without his finding out."

"How can you divorce a man you can't find?" Harriett asked reasonably.

"He's getting the divorce, not me. He has my address."

"Lovely. Shall we sell some books? Call the doctor first," Harriett said, and went back to her pricing.

Dani was healthy, and after her family doctor put her on prenatal vitamins, she began to bloom. Dr. Henry Carter laughed delightedly every visit she made to his office for checkups, pleased with her progress as well as her attitude toward being pregnant.

"You really love being pregnant, don't you?" he asked when she was having her third checkup, at a little over four and a half months.

"Every second!" She touched the swell of her abdomen. "I think he moved this morning," she added excitedly. "Little flutters, like a bird trying to get free."

"Yes," he said with a warm smile. "That's what it feels like, I'm told. The first sign of a healthy baby. The tests we ran assured us of that."

She'd liked the test—it was done with ultrasound, and they'd given her a polaroid picture of the baby's head, just visible in the X-ray–type sound scan.

"Has there been any word from your husband?" he added quietly.

Dani felt herself go cold. "No." She started down at her hands. "He might. . .never come back."

"I'm sorry. The reason I asked is because I'd like you to sign up for natural childbirth classes. Even if you don't want to have a natural delivery, they'll help you cope with labor," he explained. "They involve exercises that prepare you for childbirth. And, sadly, they require a partner."

"Can—can Harriett do it?" she asked.

He knew Harriett, and he grinned. "Best person I know for a coach. All she really has to do is stand beside you and tell you when to breathe."

"She already does that very well," she said dryly.

"Okay. Next month I'll sign you up. You're doing fine. Get out of here. And don't exert yourself too much. The heat's terrible this summer."

"Tell me about it," she murmured, sweating even in her loose sleeveless tent blouse and elastic-fronted skirt. "See you next time."

She made another appointment and dawdled on her way back to work. It was a lovely summer day, the kind that lures dreamers to quiet ponds and butterfly-laden meadows full of flowers. She sang a little as she walked along, feeling the tiny flutters in her stomach and laughing as she went. What a beautiful world. How wonderful to be pregnant and healthy.

Finally, she gave in and went back to the bookstore, because she knew Harriett would worry if she was gone too long. She strolled lazily along the small shopping center in the heart of Greenville, oblivious to shoppers and the sounds of children playing on the sidewalk.

With a slow, dreamy smile, she opened the door of the shop and walked inside. And came face to face with Dutch.

He was wearing khakis—a bush shirt with slacks—and there was a new scar on one cheek. He looked as though he'd lost a little weight, although he was as handsome, as physically devastating, as ever. Harriett must have thought so, too, because she was openly staring at him, wide-eyed.

Dutch did some staring of his own. His eyes were on her stomach, and their expression was frankly terrified. He felt as if he'd never breathe again. He'd come back to see if they could work out a compromise, if she might be willing to rethink her position. Only to find—this!

Dani saw the stark terror in his eyes. If she'd hoped for any kind of reconciliation, she knew now that it was all a pipe dream. After all the long nights of remembering, worrying, hoping, praying, for him, of thinking how he'd react if she told him about the baby, now she knew.

It was too much all at once. The sight of him, the hunger for him, the weeks and months of worry. He began to blur, and then to darken. And she fainted at his feet.

She came to in the back of the shop, in a storeroom that Dani and Harriett used for lunch breaks. There was a big armchair there, and Dani was lying across it, her shoes off, a cold cloth on her forehead.

"...had a hard time of it," Harriett was saying grimly. "She's healthy enough, but she won't rest."

"I never should have married her," came the harsh reply.

"You're a prize, aren't you?" Harriett was saying. "That child has never had anything or anyone in her life to make her way easier. Her parents deserted her when she was just a baby; she doesn't even know where they are. She never really had a boyfriend of her own. She's had no one except me. And now you sweep her off her feet, get her pregnant, and walk out on her. Mister, you are a walking blond plague, and if there's one iota of human decency left in you, you'll do her a favor and get out of her life."

"And leave her at your mercy?" Dutch came back idly. "Like hell."

Oh, no, Dani thought sickly. She'd known that would happen. World War III. Dutch and Harriett were just alike....

"What kind of mercy would she get from you, you...!" Harriett retorted.

"No," Dani whispered hoarsely, opening her eyes to see them squared off, glaring at each other scant feet away. They both turned toward her. "No," she repeated more strongly. "If you two want to brawl, go stand in the street. You can't do it here. I can't cope."

"I'm sorry, baby," Harriett said softly. "Are you all right?"

"I'm fine, thanks." She sat up, smoothing the wet cloth over her face while Dutch glared down at her with fierce anger in his dark eyes. His blond hair was slightly mussed, his handsome face harder than she remembered it. "Well, you needn't glare at me," she told him shortly. "I didn't get pregnant all alone, remember!"

Harriett had to hide a smile. "I'll leave you two to talk," she offered.

"We'll talk at home," Dani said firmly, glaring at Dutch. "Where I can throw things and scream. The store cramps my style."

She got up while Dutch tried not to grin at her fury. Glasses and all, she was something in a temper.

"Don't rush around; it isn't healthy," he said, taking her hand in his. He glanced at Harriett. "Can you manage for an hour or so?"

"Of course. Can you?" she returned.

He couldn't help the faint smile. "Yes, Mama," he said mockingly,. "I won't hurt your lamb."

He guided her out the door, letting her show him the way to her nearby apartment. It was up a flight of stairs, and he frowned as they climbed. He didn't like the stairs.

"You have to move," he said when she'd unlocked her apartment and they were inside in the white and yellow homey confines of the living room.

She turned and gaped at him. "What?"

"You have to move," he said shortly. "You can't be walking up and down stairs like...that." He indicated her belly.

"It isn't a that. It's a baby," she said firmly, planting her feet as she challenged him. "It's a boy, in fact, and I am going to call him Joshua Eric."

His face gave nothing away. His eyes went over her quietly, and for the first time in months he felt whole again. Leaving her had been the hardest thing he'd ever done. All the time he was away, he thought of her, longed for her, wanted her. He still wanted her. But she was pregnant. He didn't want a baby, he didn't want her pregnant. It brought back memories that were unbearable.

He hadn't even meant to come back; he hadn't wanted his life to change. And his worst fears had confronted him the instant he saw her.

"Do you have the divorce papers with you?" she asked calmly.

He sighed angrily and lit a cigarette without even asking if she minded. "You've put 'paid' to that, haven't you?" he asked, his voice as cold as his dark eyes. "How can I divorce you in that condition? You'll want child support, I imagine?"

He couldn't possibly have hurt her any more, not if he'd knocked her down. Quick tears welled in her eyes, and she glared at him through them.

"Get out!" she shot at him.

"Is it even mine?" he goaded, feeling trapped and straining at invisible bonds fiercely.

She picked up the nearest object, a small statuette of some Greek figure, and flung it at him. "Damn you!"

He ducked and it hit the door, shattering into a hundred pieces.

"Get out of my apartment! Get out of my life!" she choked. "Oh, God, I hate you, I hate—!" The nausea hit her all at once. She turned, running for the bathroom, where she was horribly sick. She cried helplessly, oblivious to the tall man holding the wet cloth to her head and hating himself so much he wanted to jump off a building to make the guilt stop.

"I hate you," she whispered weakly when it was over and she could talk. Her head was leaning against the cold porcelain sink. She could hardly move.

"Yes." He bathed her face gently, her hands. Then he put the cloth aside and lifted her, carrying her into the bedroom. He laid her down and turned on the oscillating fan, positioning it so that it wouldn't blow directly on her.

"Go to sleep," he said quietly. "Then we'll talk."

"I—don't want to," she murmured drowsily, but she was drained and overwhelmed and so tired. Her eyes closed, and seconds later she drifted off.

Dutch sat down on the bed beside her, frightened and sick at what he'd done to her. His eyes ran lovingly over her body, and without conscious thought he eased up the hem of her maternity blouse and moved the elastic of her skirt down, and looked. Her belly was slightly swollen, round and womanly. So that was what pregnancy looked like. He winced, remembering another time, another pregnant woman. But Dani wasn't like that, he told himself. Never like that. His lean fingers touched the soft flesh gently, hesitantly. Yes, it was firm. His child was in there. His child. A boy, she'd said. Could she be so certain? Of course, there were tests they did now. His big hand smoothed over the swell, pressing, and all at once something fluttered against his fingers. He jerked them back with a gasp.

Dani had woken with the first light touch of his fingers, and she found the expressions that flickered on his face fascinating. But that last reaction amused her, and she laughed softly.

His eyes darted to hers. "What did I do?" he asked softly.

"The baby moved," she said simply.

"Moved?" He looked back down, frowning. Hesitantly, he reached down again. She took his fingers and placed them against the side of her belly. She pressed them close, and it happened again. And he laughed. Slowly. Softly. Delightedly.

"When they get bigger, they kick," she told him. "The doctor says the more active they are, the healthier they are. He moves a lot."

"I never knew...." He looked up from her belly to her rib cage. His hand moved up to the bunched top and he glanced up at her face with the question in his eyes. "I've never seen a pregnant woman this way."

"I don't mind if you look at me," she whispered, fascinated by the way he was reacting to her. There was something in his face, a kind of tenderness. She wondered what had soured him on pregnancy, and why he hated the thought of a child.

He lifted the blouse to under her chin and his body stilled as his eyes sought the subtle changes in her breasts.

"You're bigger," he said quietly. "Darker...here." His fingers brushed an enlarged areole, making her tense with remembered pleasure.

"Little changes," she said, fighting for breath. "All that will increase as I get further along. It prepares me so that I can nurse him."

He felt a wild charge of emotion. It showed when he looked into her eyes. "I didn't think women did that anymore."

She smiled. "I want to do everything. I—" She laughed. "I love it. Being pregnant, I mean. I've never had anyone to fuss over, you see," she tried to explain. "Never had anyone of my own to worry about, to care about, to love. He'll be my whole world. I'll take care of him, and sit with him when he's sick, and play games with him when he's older. I'll take him everywhere with me, I'll—" She lowered her eyes at the expression on his face.

"What you said, about child support. It's not necessary," she added proudly. "I make a comfortable living from the bookstore. I can take care of him. He'll be my responsibility."

He'd never felt so empty and alone in all his life. He stared at her belly, hearing the words and wanting all that tender caring for himself. But it wasn't possible. She didn't want him. She was telling him so.

He tugged the blouse back down. "You'll be a good mother," he said numbly.

"I'm sorry that you had to find it out this way," she murmured. "I would have written you, but I didn't even have your address."

He drew in a slow breath and got to his feet. He went to the window, smoking another cigarette. He looked so alone. So lost.

"You...weren't hurt?" she asked, averting her face so that he couldn't see her eyes.

"A few scratches." He stared at the glowing tip of the cigarette for a minute before his dark eyes went back out the window to the city traffic. He'd done nothing right since he got off the damned plane. He'd wanted to talk about reconciliation, but when he'd found her pregnant, he'd gone off the deep end. It was because of the memories, of course; they'd haunted him for so long. Perhaps he'd blown the whole incident out of proportion over the years.

He turned back to her, uneasy at the way she looked. That woman, Harriett, had mentioned how tired Dani was. Yes, she was tired. Run down. There had been a radiance in her when she'd come into the bookstore, but it was gone now. He'd taken it away with his cold attitude and stupid accusations. He'd hurt her. Again. And he hadn't meant to.

"What I said, before," he said hesitantly, glancing at her. His hand, holding the cigarette, moved aimlessly. "I know the baby's mine."

"Do you?" she asked with an empty smile as she sat up. "I might have had a legion of lovers since you left."

"I came back to see if we might salvage the marriage," he said after a minute, hoping for some reaction in her face, but there was nothing.

She looked up at him, schooling her features to remain calm. "And now?"

He shifted restlessly, pacing near the window, his blond head bowed, one hand in his pocket. "Now I don't know."

She swung her feet to the floor. "I haven't changed my mind, even if you've started to change yours," she said before he could speak. She looked at him with quiet gray eyes. "It's all I can do to manage carrying the baby and running my business so that I can support him. I can't have any additional pressure right now. I hope you understand."

"You keep referring to it as a 'he,' " he said curtly.

"He is a he," she told him. "They ran some tests."

He felt odd. A son. A little boy who might look like him. He stared at her as if he'd never seen a woman before, studying every line and curve of her body.

"Don't look so worried, Eric, I don't expect anything from you," she mused, getting slowly to her feet. "Now, if you've said all you came to say, I've got to work to do. I'll give you the name of my attorney...."

"No!" The word came out without conscious volition. They couldn't divorce. Hell, he didn't even want to think about it! She had his child, and he...wanted it!

She clenched her fingers together and glared at him. "I won't live with you," she said stubbornly.

His face hardened. "You will."

"Make me."

He stared at her. Mutinous bow mouth, stormy gray eyes, flushed face. Pregnant. He started to laugh helplessly, a deep, rich sound like velvet.

"I like you," he said absently. "I honestly like you. No deceit, no tricks, no lines, no backing away from trouble. You're a hell of a woman."

She shifted from one foot to the other. No, he wasn't going to get around her that way. "Remember me?" she asked coldly. "Miss Frump?"

He put out the cigarette, still smiling faintly, and moved toward her with a gleam in his eyes that made her back away.

"Sexy frump," he murmured dryly. "Very pregnant, very desirable. And I don't want a divorce. I want you."

"I'm not for sale," she told him, moving backward until the wall stopped her. "Go away. Go blow up something."

"I don't blow up things, actually," he murmured, pinning her to the wall with a strong arm on either side of her. "I'm more into logistics and strategy."

"You'll get killed, anyway," she said.

He shrugged. "I could get hit by a car downstairs."

"Not quite as easily," she argued.

"I want you," he said quietly.

"Yes, I know," she replied softly. "But wanting isn't enough. You've already said you'd never fall in love again, so all you're offering me is your body, between wars. It's a gorgeous body, and in bed you're all any woman could ever want. But you're asking me to live with death, day in and day out, and I can't."

He drew in a breath and started to speak, but before he could she took one of his hands and pressed it slowly against her belly.

"I have your son under my heart," she whispered, pressing his palm flat against her. "I can't live with the fear of losing both of you."

He frowned. "I don't understand."

"Eric, I could miscarry," she said, her voice soft with a fear he was just beginning to sense.

"Is it likely?" he asked.

"I'm healthy. So is the baby. But there are no guarantees," she said, lowering her eyes to his chest.

"It…frightens you, to think of losing him?" he asked hesitantly.

She looked up wide-eyed. "Of course it does!"

He was remembering another woman, another time, and he cursed himself for that lapse. Dani wanted the baby. It was written all over her.

"I can't worry about him and you as well," she said curtly. "And he deserves a chance. You're old enough to make your own mistakes, but I'm responsible for him now."

He stared down at her for a long time. Then he turned away with a sigh and lit still another cigarette.

"I've done it for so many years," he said after a minute, staring at the floor. "It's all I know."

"I'm not asking you to change," she reminded him.

He looked up. "We're married."

"We can get divorced."

"I don't want a damned divorce!" he burst out, his eyes black with anger.

She stood there staring at him helplessly, searching for the right words.

He sighed angrily. "I knew you'd be trouble the minute I saw you," he growled. "A frumpy little bookseller with the body and soul of an angel. And you're in my blood like poison. I'd have to die to get you out of my system!''

She lifted her shoulders and smiled ruefully. "Well, look at it this way, you'll never have to fight off other men."

He laughed softly, shaking his head. "Would you care to bet? The way you look right now..."

"I look pregnant," she said. "In two or three more months I'll look like a blimp."

"Not to me you won't."

He averted his eyes to his shoes. "Well, I'll go home and pack. And there are some people I want to see."

"Pack?"

He looked up. "I'm going to live with you," he said. "If you don't like it, that's tough. I am not," he continued, gathering steam, "going to have you working yourself to death and running up and down these damned stairs. Harriett's right. You need looking after. So I'm going to look after you. Until the baby comes, at least," he added. "After that we'll make whatever decisions have to be made."

She wanted to argue. But he looked very formidable. "But, your...your work...."

"To hell with my work," he bit off. He looked frankly dangerous. "I've got enough in foreign banks to buy this damned building you live in. I work because I like it, not because I need money."

"But..."

"Shh. Talking is bad for the baby." He crushed out his cigarette. "I'll get back Saturday."

Things were happening too fast. She was shell-shocked. She watched him walk toward her.

"Little gray-eyed witch," he whispered. He pulled her gently against him and bent to tease her mouth with his. "Open it," he murmured. "I haven't kissed you in months."

"I'll bet you've kissed other women," she said mutinously.

He lifted his head. "Nope." He drew his knuckles over her flushed cheek. "I haven't even looked at one. And yes, there are always women in the circles I move in. Beautiful women, with no principles and eyes like dollar signs. And all I could think of was how it felt with you, that morning when we made such exquisite love on my bed and created this little boy."

Tears burst into her eyes, startling him. "You know?" she breathed.

"Of course. Didn't you?" he asked, smiling at her.

"You're more experienced than I am," she hedged.

"Not in that kind of lovemaking," he murmured ruefully. "I wasn't lying when I said I'd never experienced it before."

"Do you mind very much, about the baby?" she asked, because she had to know.

He smoothed away her frown with a lean forefinger. "I have to get used to the idea, that's all.

I've been a free spirit for a very long time. I've had no one."

"Yes, I know." She studied his shirt buttons. "Eric, you don't have to do this. You don't have to come here...."

He stopped the sacrificing little speech with his mouth, opening hers to a delicate, gently probing kiss that had her going stiff with desire all too soon.

His fingers tangled in the short hair at the nape of her neck and eased her head back against the hard muscle of his upper arm. His other hand made slow, torturous forays against her collarbone, her shoulder, the side of her breast.

"Sadist," she whispered shakily as the magic worked on her.

He bit her lower lip gently. "Do you want to make love?"

Her eyes opened, looking straight into his face. "No."

He smiled, and his fingers brushed knowingly over her nipples. She flinched with sudden pleasure, and he laughed gently.

"Yes, you do," he murmured dryly.

"My mind doesn't want to," she amended, trying to save herself from the sensual prison he was trying to trap her in.

He kissed her eyes closed, and his hands slid to her stomach, cupping its firm warmth. "It won't make you miscarry," he whispered. "Not if I'm gentle enough. And I will be."

She trembled at the soft tone, and he smiled and pulled her into his arms, holding her.

"It isn't that," she whispered into his shoulder, eyes open and worried as they stared at the fabric of his shirt. "Don't make me care for you. It will make it all that much harder to let go. Just...just let me pretend that it's Mexico, and we're having a holiday. All right?"

He stood very still, smoothing her hair. "Dani..."

"Please!"

He sighed heavily and let her go. "All right. A holiday." His eyes dropped to her belly and he chuckled. "For the three of us."

"And—and no sex," she added, her eyes dark and frightened.

He searched them, seeing her fear of losing him. It bothered him, but he didn't quite know how to handle it. "Are you sure?" he asked. "We could enjoy each other."

"Yes, I know. But I don't want to."

She was imposing impossible limits on his self-control, but he couldn't turn his back on his responsibility to her. He shrugged, as if it didn't matter. "Okay," he said carelessly. "No sex."

She breathed more easily. She had expected him to argue. He brushed a kiss against her nose.

"Of course," he added, "you can always seduce me if you like."

"Thank you," she replied with a reluctant smile. "I'll keep that in mind."

He winked at her. "See you Saturday. Rest for another hour. I'll stop by your store and tell the mother hen where you are. And watch those damned stairs," he added firmly.

"Yes, your worship." She curtsied.

He laughed shortly as he went out the door, closing it quietly behind him. Dani stared at it for a long time before she went back to lie down. She wondered what she was letting herself in for. He wasn't going to be able to settle down, she was sure of it. It would mean only more heartache. But apparently he felt responsible and he wasn't going to let her out of his sight for five months. She grimaced at the thought of having to cope with Dutch and Harriett together. It was going to be a rough pregnancy.

Eight

Dutch thought that getting married might have been worth it all when he saw the shock on J.D.'s and Gabby's faces.

J.D. Brettman was big and dark. He was an ex-mercenary who now practiced law in Chicago. And Gabby Darwin Brettman had been his secretary before she married him. Dutch had heard a little about her from First Shirt, another member of the team, who'd told him how rough the courtship had been, and he'd met her once himself. Now he need advice, and he couldn't think of anyone better than J.D. to ask.

"Married." J.D. caught his breath. "You?"

Dutch shrugged. He looked up from his lit cigarette to catch the amused look in Gabby's green eyes, and he laughed in spite of himself. "It's your fault," he told her. "I never would have noticed her, but for you. Until J.D. married you, I thought all women were incapable of honesty."

J.D. touched Gabby's cheek gently. "She changed my own outlook," he said, and a look passed between them that embarrassed Dutch.

Dutch got up and went to the window, staring blankly out at Chicago. "I don't know what to do," he confessed. "I thought I would keep working and we'd each have our own lives. But she won't agree to that. She says she can't handle knowing what I'm doing when I'm away."

J.D. got up. "I'll make a pot of coffee. Gabby, keep Dutch company, will you?"

"Sure." She got up and went to the window, standing quietly beside the tall blond man, her arms folded over her chest. She looked at him. "I was going to get out of J.D.'s life when I thought he might go back to it," she said honestly. "I couldn't handle it, either." Her shoulders rose and fell. "I'm not a coward, but the worry would have made one of me. If he'd been a policeman or worked in law enforcement, I suppose I'd have had to make the best of it. But the kind of work he did, and you do, isn't easy for a woman to cope with. It's extraordinarily dangerous."

"Gabby," he said, staring out the window, "how would you have felt if J.D. hadn't been able to give it up—and you were pregnant?"

Tears burst from her eyes. He looked down and saw them, and his face contorted. "Oh, God," he breathed roughly.

She turned away. "I'm sorry," she said. "I want a baby so much. But J.D. and I haven't been able to have one. If I were pregnant, and he went off to a war, I think I'd die in my sleep."

He started to speak and couldn't. He lifted the cigarette to his lips, anguish in his eyes.

"I meant to tell you," J.D. said minutes later, after he'd brought the coffee, "that Apollo's been cleared of any criminal charges."

"You got him off?" Dutch asked with a smile, feeling happy for their old friend and comrade.

J.D. nodded. "It took a little work. But he was innocent; that helped." He pursed his lips and glanced at Dutch. "He's opened his own business."

"Oh? Doing what?" Dutch asked.

"A consulting firm. He specializes in teaching anti-terrorism tactics to international corporations. And already he's got more work than he can handle." He leaned back against the sofa. "It's exciting work. Even a little risky. He asked if you might be interested. He needs someone experienced in tactics and strategy."

"A desk job," Dutch scoffed.

"Not at all. Go see him."

Dutch met J.D.'s level gaze. "I don't know if I can settle down."

"I didn't know, either." He glanced at Gabby, who was writing letters at the small desk, her long hair around her shoulders. "But it wasn't hard to decide which meant more, a few wild thrills, or her. She's my world," he added in a tone that made Dutch look away.

He leaned forward, staring at the carpet. "Dani's pregnant."

J.D. hesitated. "Is it yours?"

He nodded and smiled. "No doubt about it."

Later, he went to see Apollo Blain, the tall black man who'd been part of their small unit since J.D. and First Shirt had formed it years ago. Apollo grinned at him from behind his big desk, looking urbane and capable and prosperous.

"Tired of planning battles?" Apollo chuckled as he shook Dutch's outstretched hand. "Help me save paunchy executives from terrorists. It's a hell of a lot safer, and the pay's good."

"J.D. said I might like it," Dutch sighed, settling back in an armchair. "I got married."

"You?" Apollo gaped at him. He felt his own forehead. "My God, I must have an awful fever. I thought you just said you were married."

"I am. And I've got a son on the way," came the amused reply.

"I'd better lie down."

"Not until we discuss this job," Dutch returned.

"Are you really interested?" Apollo asked seriously.

Dutch nodded. "I don't know if I can stick it out. That's up front. But I think I need to try, for her sake."

Apollo whistled. "I'd like to meet this lady. Anything like Gabby?"

Dutch smiled. "Quite a lot."

"I hope there aren't any more of them running around loose." Apollo shuddered. "Even First Shirt's on the verge, with Gabby's mother. Anyway, enough about that. Here's what I had in mind, if you'd like to give it a shot...."

Dutch lit a cigarette and listened quietly. He nodded. Yes, it sounded like an interesting job. Outwitting terrorists. He smiled. Perhaps he might even enjoy it. He leaned back and crossed his legs as Apollo's deep voice outlined the project.

When Dani told her best friend what was happening, Harriett had little to say about it, except to mutter something about a strong cage and a thin whip.

"He's not at all difficult when you know him." Dani grinned impishly. "And you have to admit, he's rather extraordinarily handsome."

"Handsome doesn't have anything to do with it," Harriett said curtly. And then she smiled. And growled wolfishly. And went off grinning.

Dani stared after Harriett, her own smile being slowly replaced by a frown. Her hand went absently to the swell of her stomach and she walked back behind the counter slowly.

It all seemed like a dream, somehow. The only reality left in her life was the baby. How in the world was she going to cope with a husband who felt trapped? She couldn't forget the look on his face when he'd seen that she was pregnant, couldn't forget what he'd said to her. He'd apologized, but still she couldn't forget. He didn't want this baby for some reason, and although he desired Dani, he didn't love her. His feelings were superficial at best, nothing that a marriage could be built on.

Her eyes went to the order sheet on the counter and she stared at it blankly, oblivious to the sound of Harriett helping a new customer find the books she wanted. Harriett had been right; she should have kept her head in Mexico. How incredible that level headed Dani had gone off the deep end and married a stranger. It wasn't like her.

And now he felt responsible for what he'd done, and he was going to take care of her. She almost cried. Not because he loved her, but because the baby was his fault. She stared at her neat, short nails. How could she bear seeing him day after day, knowing that only the baby held him to her, that when it was all over, he'd be gone again. Perhaps he'd be killed. Her eyes closed in agony.

"Stop it," Harriett whispered sharply, pausing by the counter. "Stop tormenting yourself. At least he cares enough to look after you, doesn't he?"

Her eyelids lifted, and her anguished gray eyes were fogged from tears. "Does he?"

"He was snarling like a mountain lion," Harriett said, "when he stopped by here on this way to the airport. But it wasn't all guilt, you know. He's really worried about you."

Dani sighed thoughtfully. "He was terrified when he saw I was pregnant, Harrie," she murmured. "And when we got back to my apartment...he said some harsh things."

"None of which he meant, I imagine." Harriett patted her hand. "But you've got to stop worrying. It isn't healthy."

"He said he had to see some people," Dani said tightly.

"So that's it." Harriett glanced toward the browsing customer. "If he said he'd be back, he will. You can't put a rope around a man like that."

"I'd die if I lost him," she whispered, closing her eyes. "I offered him a divorce, and he wouldn't take it. I can't bear being nothing more than a responsibility."

"Once he gets to know you, that might change. Have you thought of it that way?" Harriett asked with a quiet smile. "Now, get busy. That's the best therapy I know for worry. Okay?"

"Okay." But as the days went by, the worries grew. What if he didn't come back at all? What if the people he was seeing told him of another mission, and he couldn't resist taking it?

Friday afternoon, when she left, she asked Harriett to open up the next morning so that she could sleep late. She was tired, and the worry wasn't helping. Harriett started to say something, but apparently thought better of it.

Something woke Dani. A movement beside her, a heavy weight on the bed. She came awake slowly, her face pale and drawn from lack of rest, her eyes heavily shadowed.

Dutch stared at her with unconcealed anxiety. She looked even worse than when he'd left. His eyes went slowly down her body to the swell of her stomach and they darkened. He didn't touch her this time. She didn't want that, he recalled bitterly, she didn't want him in any physical way anymore.

Dani blinked and almost reached out to touch him. Was he real? Her eyes wandered over his broad shoulders in the tan raincoat he was wearing. His blond hair was damp, too, curling a little around the sides of his face, and she wondered if their child would inherit that slight waviness.

"I didn't expect you so early," she said drowsily. "Is it raining?"

"Cats and dogs." He stood up, moving away from the bed. "Harriett's watching the store, I gather?"

"Yes. Would you like some breakfast?" she asked, although the thought of food was giving her problems already.

"I had it on the plane," he said. He lit a ciga-rette and glanced at her. "Can you eat anything?"

She shook her head. "Not now, I can't. I have toast when I get up."

"I'll go make some."

She gaped at him, and he laughed reluctantly.

"Well, I can toast bread, you know," he said. "We used to take turns with chow when the group and I were on a mission."

Her eyes lowered quickly to the bedspread. She touched the design in the white chenille. "The. . .people you had to see?" Her glance skipped to his hard face and down again. "I'm sorry. That's none of my business." She got up, standing slowly because any movement could trigger the nausea.

He felt as if he'd taken a hard blow in the stom-ach. Not her business! For God's sake, didn't she even care?

He turned, striding angrily into the kitchen while she sighed miserably, wondering what she'd done, and made her way into the bathroom.

The toast was on the table when she joined him. She'd thrown on a sleeveless flowered dress and came barefoot into the room, her hair gently brushed, her face white and drawn. He was wear-ing jeans and a brown knit shirt that made him look even more vital, tanned and powerful than usual.

"Thank you," she said as she sat down.

"You don't look well," he said bluntly.

"I'm pregnant."

"Yes, I noticed that."

She looked up and caught an amused gleam in his dark eyes.

"I don't ever feel well in the morning," she returned. "It's normal. And as for looking well," she added with a glare, "as you like to remind me, I never have looked well. I'm frumpy."

"Talk about bad moods," he murmured, leaning back to smoke his cigarette with an amused smile on his firm mouth. "Eat your toast, little shrew."

She glared at him. "You don't have to feel responsible for me," she said coldly. "I've already told you, it isn't necessary for you to stay here. I can have the baby all by myself."

"Sure you can," he scoffed, his eyes narrowing. "That's why you look so healthy."

"I'd be healthier if you'd go away!" she shot back. She left the toast, started to get up and suddenly sat down again, swallowing rapidly.

Dutch went to fetch a damp cloth and held it to her face, her throat, her mouth, kneeling beside her.

"All right now?" he asked in a tone so tender, it brought quick tears to her eyes.

"Yes," she whispered miserably.

His hand sought her belly and pressed there protectively. "This is mine," he said softly, holding her gaze. "I put it there. And until it's born, and the danger is all over, I'm going to stay with you."

The tears overwhelmed her. "Oh, please go away," she whispered brokenly. "Please..."

He pulled her gently against him, her face against his, his arms warm and strong at her back. He smelled of spicy cologne and cigarette smoke, and her body reacted to him with a crazy surge of pleasure that she tried to fight down. It wasn't permanent, she had to keep reminding herself, it was only temporary, until the baby was born. She'd better not get too attached to the feel of his arms.

"I was going to wait until later to discuss this with you," he said after a minute, "but I think we'd better talk now. Come here."

He lifted her in his arms and stood up in one smooth motion, carrying her back into the bedroom.

He laid her down against the pillows and leaned over her, searching her wide gray eyes behind the glasses.

"You're killing me," she whispered achingly.

"I can see that," he said quietly. "It isn't making my life any easier. I can't love you," he said tersely, and his face was hard. "I'm sorry. I'm...very fond of you," he added, brushing the tears from her cheeks. He took off her glasses and laid them aside, wiping the tear tracks away with a corner of the sheet. "But what there was in me of love died long ago. I can't afford the luxury of caring, not in my line of work."

Her eyes closed and her voice was hoarse with pain. "I love you," she said helplessly, her voice strained.

"I know," he replied. Her eyes opened, and he searched them. What the hell! She needed to know. Perhaps it would help her to understand. He took a sharp breath. "The woman, the one I loved so desperately...she became pregnant with my child," he said coldly. "The day she left me she told me she'd had an abortion. She laughed about it. How absurd, she said, to think that she'd want a child of mine!" His hands gripped her arms fiercely, but she didn't notice it at all. Her shocked eyes were fixed on his tortured face. "She got rid of it," he said harshly, "like so much garbage!"

Now she understood. Now it all made sense. She reached up hesitantly and touched his face.

"I'm raw from thinking about it," he whispered roughly, "from the memories. When I saw you pregnant with my child it all came back like a fever." His eyes blazed. "You don't know me. What I am now, she made me..."

Her fingers touched his hard mouth, feeling its warmth. Everything soft and womanly inside her reached out. Poor, storm-battered man, she thought achingly. Poor, tortured man.

"My parents hated me," he ground out. "They died hating me!"

"Come here." She reached up, drawing him down with her, holding him. He shuddered, and her eyes closed. Perhaps he didn't love her, but he needed her. She knew that even if he didn't. Her arms enfolded him—loving, comforting arms. Her hands smoothed his cool blond hair, and she nuzzled her cheek against it.

"Parents never hate children," she said quietly. "Not really."

"How would you know?" he growled harshly. "Didn't yours desert you?"

She took a slow breath, clinging to him. "Yes." She shifted under his formidable weight. "They were very young. Just children themselves. The responsibility must have been terrible." She held him closer. "They tried to contact me once. My aunt...told them I was dead." He stiffened and she swallowed hard. "I found out only when she was dying herself. It was too late then."

"Dani..."

"We can't go back, either of us," she continued quietly. Her hand brushed the nape of his neck. "We have to do the best we can with what we have."

"Are you sorry that I made you pregnant?" he asked in a tone so quiet she barely heard it.

"I've already told you that I'm happy," she said, and smiled against his cool skin. "I've never had anyone of my own."

It was a long minute before he lifted his head. He drew in a slow, calming breath and met her eyes.

His own were stormy, turbulent; his face was terrible with remembered pain.

"I would never hurt you," she said. "Never, in any way, even if I had the ability. She was a horrible woman, and you were young and vulnerable. But I'm sure your parents understood, even if they were hurt. And I will never believe that they didn't love you," she said, her face soft and caring.

His jaw tautened. He got to his feet and turned away. A long moment later he fumbled to light a cigarette.

Dani, blind without her glasses, didn't see the betraying movement of his hands. She tugged her glasses back on and sat up, straightening her dress, which had ridden up her legs.

"I have to get to the store," she said after the long silence began to grate on her nerves. "Harriett has an appointment to get her hair cut at noon."

He turned, scowling. "You're in no condition to go to work," he said curtly.

She looked up, eyebrows raised. "Fudge! I'm a little shaky on my legs, that's all." She got up, daring him to stop her. "I've got a business to take care of."

"You've got a baby to take care of," he corrected. "Call Harriett and tell her to close up when she leaves."

She glared at him. "No."

He shrugged and watched her pull out a slip and hose, and she thought the matter was settled.

He waited until she started to pull the dress over her head. Then he put down his cigarette and moved forward. Before she had time to react he stripped her, quickly and deftly, and put her under the covers. Then he took her clothes, tossed them into the closet, locked the closet, and pocketed the key.

She lay there with the covers around her neck, staring at him with eyes like saucers. It had happened so quickly, she'd had not time to retaliate.

He picked up the phone and asked for the number of her bookstore. Blankly, she told him. He finished dialing.

"Harriett? This is Dutch. Dani said to close up the shop when you leave. She's staying in bed today. Yes, that's right. Yes, I will." He hung up and retrieved his cigarette. "Now," he told Dani, "you'll stay right there until I say you can get up."

"I won't!" she returned.

"All right," he said easily, sliding one hand into his pocket. "Get up."

She started to, remembered her unclothed condition, and sank back against the pillows. "I want my clothes."

"You can have them tomorrow."

"I want them now."

"Go back to sleep. It's only nine," he said. "I'll clean up the kitchen.

He started out of the room and she stared at him uncomprehendingly, her eyes wide and uncertain. He turned and looked at her, the cigarette in his hand sending up curls of gray smoke.

"You're very much like Gabby," he said quietly.

He was gone before she could reply. Was Gabby the woman in his past? she wondered miserably. She took off her glasses and turned her face into her pillow as fresh tears came. She was sure that he hated her. Why else would he have said such a thing to her?

Eventually, she slept. It was late afternoon when she awoke, to find her clothes at the foot of the bed and a note under the pillow. Drowsily, she unfolded the paper and read it.

You can have your clothes, but don't leave the apartment, it said in a bold black scrawl. *I have gone to do some shopping. Back by five. Dutch.*

She glanced at the clock beside the bed. It was almost five now. She scrambled out of bed quickly to dress before he got back.

When he came in, with a bag of groceries in one powerful arm, she was curled up on the sofa with her ledgers spread around her. He glared and she glared back.

"Well, somebody has to do the paperwork," she said stubbornly. "And you won't let me do my job."

"Tit for tat," he said carelessly. "You won't let me do mine."

"I won't get killed selling books," she returned.

"I like the idea of being a father now that I'm getting used to it," he said as he put down the bag on the kitchen table. "I'm not going to let you risk losing him."

"You make me sound as if I didn't care about him at all," she snapped.

He started putting food into the refrigerator. "Stop trying to pick fights with me," he said pleasantly. "I won't argue with you."

"I'm not picking a fight," she said tautly. She just found it hard to believe that he was really concerned about her. She put her paperwork aside and padded into the kitchen to get something cold to drink. The heat was stifling, and the little air conditioner in the window was barely adequate.

He turned, frowning at her damp skin. "Are you hot?" he asked gently. "I'll get a bigger air conditioner delivered."

"No, you won't," she said stubbornly. "I like the one I've got."

He took her by the arms and held her in front of him. "You won't win," he said quietly. "So stop trying. I have to go to Chicago on Monday."

She wouldn't look up. "Work?" she asked, trying to sound as if she didn't care.

"Work," he agreed. His hands smoothed up and down her soft arms. "I'm not making any promises."

"Have I asked for any?" she murmured, lifting her eyes.

"You wouldn't," he said, as if he knew. "You're too proud to ask for anything that isn't freely given." He bent and started to kiss her, but she turned her face away.

He felt a tremor of hurt and anger go through him. His hands clenched, and he moved away from her with a new and unexpected pain eating at him.

He sighed angrily. How the hell had she gotten so far under his skin? He wanted to throw things.

"I'm not leaving the country," he said curtly. "An old friend of mine has opened a consulting firm. He teaches counterterrorism tactics to corporate executives. He needed someone experienced in tactics, and asked if I'd be interested." He shrugged. "So I told him yes."

It shocked her that he'd even consider changing his profession. Did the baby mean so much? Yes, she thought, probably it did. There were deep scars on his heart. Perhaps he'd never truly get over them. She didn't have the beauty or the sophistication to capture his heart. It wasn't enough that he desired her. Desire was something a man could feel for almost anybody, frumpy or not.

"It's a long way to commute," she said quietly.

"Yes." He moved toward her, but this time he didn't come too close. He studied her, and she looked back, noticing how very tall he was, how powerfully built. He had a face a movie star would have envied—even features, dark velvet eyes, chiseled lips.

"We discussed this a long time ago," he said. "I don't mind commuting. I think it's best, for now, that you stay here. You'd be alone a good bit of the time in Chicago, although I'm sure Gabby wouldn't mind looking in on you."

"Gabby?" She stared at him.

"Gabby Brettman," he said. "She's married to one of my best friends, a trial lawyer." His firm mouth relaxed into a smile. "Gabby followed J.D. through a Central American jungle with an AK-47 under one arm. She actually shot a terrorist with it and saved his life. A hell of a woman, Gabby."

So Gabby hadn't been the woman from his past! And he admired her—he'd said that Dani was much like Gabby. She blushed.

"Now you make the connection, is that it?" he asked softly. "For God's sake, what did you think I meant when I compared you to her?"

Her eyes fell to his chest. "I thought...she was the woman who betrayed you," she said miserably, and went back to the sofa.

"You don't read me any better than I read you," he said after a minute. "Suppose you come to Chicago with me for a few days? Meet my friends. Learn a little about me."

The invitation excited her, but she hesitated. "I don't know."

"My apartment has two bedrooms," he said icily. "You won't have to sleep with me."

"I can't imagine why you'd want to," she laughed bitterly, curling up on the sofa with her ledgers. "There are a lot of pretty women in the...Eric!"

He was beside her, over her, the ledgers scattered onto the floor as he pinned her down. His eyes glittered, his chest rose and fell harshly. He held her wrists over her head and looked as if he could do her violence.

"I'd never do that to you," he said harshly. "Never! What kind of man do you think I am!"

Tears stung her eyes. "You're hurting me," she whispered unsteadily.

He loosened her wrists, but he didn't let go of them. "I'm sorry," he muttered, still glaring into her white face. "I've hardly done anything else, have I? I picked you up, got you pregnant, forced you into marriage without telling you the truth about myself...and lately all I've done is blame you for it."

Her eyes closed. The tears ran from beneath her lids, and he caught his breath.

"Don't cry," he said with reluctant concern. "Dani, don't cry. I'm sorry. *Lieveling*, I'm sorry, I'm sorry..." he told her over and over again, his mouth searching across her wet cheek to her mouth. He took it gently, opening it to the moist possession of his own, while his hands freed her wrists and moved to cup her face. "*Lieveling*," he breathed against her mouth. His body stretched full length over hers, his forearms catching the bulk of his weight. His heart pounded, his breath came unevenly. He wanted her. He wanted her!

She felt him begin to tremble, and against her hips she felt the helpless reaction of his body to her soft yielding. She hadn't wanted this to happen; she hadn't wanted to give in to something purely physical. But it had been months since she'd known the possession of that hard, expert body, and his mouth was driving her mad with its taunting hunger. She reached up hesitantly and slid her arms around his neck.

"Let me have you, Dani," he murmured into her open mouth. He shifted so that his hands could ease up her dress. "Let me have you."

She wanted to stop. But his hands were touching her soft body now, teasing it into reckless abandon, his mouth probing hers in a kiss so deep it became an act of intimacy in itself. Her body moved against his, her hands trembled and clenched on his shoulders and she moaned.

"Yes," he said, his voice urgent now, shaking. "Yes."

"Here...?" she managed in a last attempt at sanity.

"Here," he groaned, pressing her into the cushions with the gentle, carefully controlled weight of his body. "Here...!"

It was as it had been that morning in Mexico. He was breathlessly tender with her, each motion slow and sweet and reverent. His hands trembled as they touched her, guided her. His voice was passionate as he reverted to Dutch, whispering in her ear.

His mouth moved to hers, open and tender and trembling on her own as he began with aching tenderness to possess her.

Her mouth opened, her eyes widened. "Eric...!"

"Shhh," he whispered huskily. He watched her as he moved, tender motions that wouldn't harm his child, arousing motions that made her gray eyes dilate, that made her heart beat wildly against his hair-matted chest.

"Oh!" she cried out, a whisper of sound that he took into his mouth.

"Gentle violence," he said into her parted lips. "Rock with me. Take my body, and give me yours. Be my lover now."

"I...love you!" she whimpered helplessly. "I love you!"

It shattered what little was left of his control, to hear her cry it out so huskily, to see it in her eyes as she looked at him with all the barriers down. His mouth crushed softly into hers and his hands held her. He heard her fluttering little cries, felt the wildness in her body, the heat of it burning his hands. He wanted to look, but it was happening for him, too, the tender explosions that were so much more terrible than the fierce passion he'd known before with women. He thought he might die....

He was aware of her in every cell as they lay trembling together in the aftermath. His hands stroked along her relaxed body, feeling its softness in a kind of dazed reality.

"Dani?" he whispered as his eyes opened and he saw the back of the sofa.

"Yes." Her voice sounded like velvet.

"I...didn't meant to do it," he said hesitantly. "I didn't plan it."

"I know." She kissed him. Her lips touched his eyes, his eyebrows, his straight nose, his cheeks, his mouth, his chin.

He loved the softness of her mouth on his face. His eyes closed, so that she could kiss his eyelids, too. He smiled, feeling sated, loved. Profound, he thought dizzily. This, with her, was so much more than a brief merging of bodies. His hands touched her belly and felt his child move.

He laughed softly, delightedly. "He kicks," he whispered. "No more bird flutters."

"He's very strong, the doctor says," she whispered back.

He lifted his head and looked at her, at the tiny line of freckles over her nose. Sometime in the last feverish few minutes her glasses had been removed. He glanced around and saw them on the coffee table and smiled.

"I'd forgotten where we were." He sighed, kissing her again. His hands slid up her sides, and his thumbs moved over her breasts, feeling their swollen softness. "Will you let me watch you nurse him?" he asked lazily, and laughed when she blushed. "Will you?"

"Yes," she said, and buried her red face against his throat.

He kissed her forehead, her closed eyes. "Dani, is it gentle explosions for you, the way it is for me?" he asked hesitantly. "Do you feel what the French call the little death when the moment comes?"

Her breath caught. "Yes," she whispered. She clung to him. "I didn't know..."

"It was never like that for me," he told her softly, and his arms slid further around her. "Never, with anyone, the way it is with you." He shuddered.

Yes, but it was only physical, she thought miserably, and closed her eyes. Still, it was better than nothing. She smoothed the hair at his nape. It was a start.

They went to Chicago on Monday, after Dutch had taken time to call Dr. Carter to make sure it was safe for Dani to make the trip. He watched her closely, with narrowed dark eyes, every step she took. It was almost amusing, the care he was taking of her. Amusing...and very flattering. Perhaps he was growing fond of her, at least.

He hadn't loved her again. Afterward, he'd been protective and gentle, but he hadn't touched her as a lover. She wondered why, but she didn't provoke him by asking. She'd long since decided to take one day at a time, to accept what he could give without asking for more. Somehow she'd learn to live with him. Because she couldn't leave him now.

Nine

Dani wasn't sure what she'd expected Dutch's friends to look like. But when she was introduced to J.D. and Gabby Brettman and Apollo Blain, her face must have given her away.

"Yep—" Apollo nodded as he shook her shyly outstretched hand "—I told you, J.D., she expected us to look like the cover of *Soldier of Fortune* magazine."

Dani blushed and burst out laughing. "Well, I've never seen professional mercenaries before," she explained. "Anyway, at least I didn't come in looking for camouflage netting, did I?" she asked reasonably.

Apollo chuckled. "Nope, little mama, I guess not."

She lowered her eyes with a self-conscious smile, feeling Dutch's arm come around her shoulders.

"Animals." Gabby glared at the men. "Shame on you."

"Well, we're curious," J.D. said defensively. He studied Dani through eyes as dark as Dutch's. All three men were wearing lightweight suits, and Gabby was in a green-patterned dress. Dani felt as though she stood out like a sort thumb in her maternity garb.

"Of course we are," Apollo seconded. "After all, it took some kind of woman to catch Dutch, didn't it?"

"I won't argue with that." Gabby grinned. "Come on, Dani, you can help me in the kitchen while these three talk shop."

"I think I'd better," Dani confided, throwing an impish smile at Dutch. "At least I know a potato from a head of lettuce, even if I don't know an AK-47 from an Uzi."

Dutch smiled at her, possession in his whole look.

She followed Gabby into the kitchen. "What can I do?" Dani asked helpfully.

"You can tell me how you did it!" Gabby burst out delightedly, smiling from a radiant face. "Dutch, married! Honestly, J.D. and I almost fainted!"

"It's a long story," Dani murmured dryly, sensing a comrade in Gabby. She sat down at the kitchen table. "It isn't love, though, you know," she added quietly.

Gabby studied her. "For you it is. Yes, it shows. Are you happy with him?"

"As happy as I can expect to be," Dani said. "I can't hope to hold him, of course. He's very protective, and he wants the baby. But it isn't in him to love."

Gabby poured two cups of coffee, checked the timer on her microwave and sat back down. She pushed a mug of black coffee toward Dani and offered the cream and sugar.

"You know about Melissa?" she asked after a minute.

Dani knew instinctively whom she meant. "The woman from his past?"

Gabby nodded. "I wouldn't know, but Dutch was badly wounded once, and he blurted out the whole story to J.R. Dutch doesn't know," she added, lifting her eyes to Dani's. "J.D. didn't let on. But that woman...!"

"He told me all of it," Dan said quietly, sipping her coffee. "He was devastated when he found out I was pregnant."

"Did you know what he did for a living when you married him?" Gabby asked.

Dani smiled ruefully and shook her head. "I found out when the airplane we were coming home on was hijacked."

Gabby forced air through her lips. "What an interesting way to find out."

"Yes." She lowered her eyes to her cup. "He thought we could make a go of it, each leading our own lives. I didn't. I walked off and left him." She sighed. "Several weeks later I learned that I was pregnant. He came back...." She laughed. "We've been going around and around ever since."

"I remember the first time I ever heard of Dutch," Gabby recalled. "J.D.'s sister Martina had been captured by terrorists and we went to Italy to see about the ransom. Dutch was J.D.'s go-between." She looked up. "J.D. wouldn't even introduce me to him. He said Dutch hated women."

"He told me so," Dani said, smiling. "When did you get to meet him?"

"At the wedding, when I married J.D. He wasn't at all what I expected. At first I was a little nervous around him," Gabby said. "Then I got to know him—as well as he lets outsiders know him." She held Dani's curious eyes. "He talked to me about you when he was here before. He wanted to know how I'd feel if I were pregnant and J.D. couldn't give up the old life. I cried."

Dani drew in a shaky breath. "I've done my share of crying. I don't know what to do. I don't feel that I have the right to ask him to change his life for me. But I can't live with what he does." Her eyes were wide with fear and love. "I'm crazy about him. I'd die if anything happened to him."

"That's how I feel about J.D.," Gabby said quietly. "I envy you that baby," she added with a sad smile. "J.D. and I have tried..." Her thin shoulders rose and fell. "I can't seem to get pregnant."

"I had a girlfriend who couldn't get pregnant at first," Dani said, recalling an old friend from years past. She grinned. "Five years after she got married she had triplets, followed by twins the next year."

Gabby burst out laughing. "What a delightful prospect!"

"What's all the noise in here?" J.D. asked, opening the kitchen door. "Are we eating tonight?" he asked Gabby.

She got up and kissed him tauntingly on his hard mouth. "Yes, we're eating tonight, bottomless pit. And we're laughing about triplets."

His eyes widened. "What?"

"Tell you later. Let's eat!"

It was late when Dani and Dutch got back to his elegant lakeside apartment. She hadn't expected such luxury, and it emphasized once again the difference between her life-style and his. During dinner the conversation had inevitably gone back to old times and comrades whose names Dani didn't recognize. And then mention was made of the new job Apollo had offered Dutch, and Dani listened with wide eyes as it was outlined. It wasn't as dangerous as what he was doing now, of course, she reminded herself. There wasn't half the risk. She'd have to get used to it. She could, too, if she tried.

"I don't think I can manage a desk job," he told her as if he sensed her deep, frightening thoughts.

She turned from the window, where she was watching the lights of cars far below, and the city lights near the river. "Yes, I know that."

He looked at her for a long time, hands in his pockets, eyes narrow and dark and searching. "But I'm going to try."

She nodded. "I won't ask you for anything more than that," she said then. "I'll settle for whatever you can give me. I...have very little pride left." She sighed and she seemed to age. "I'd like to go to bed now, Eric. I'm so tired."

"It's been a long day. You can have whichever bedroom you like."

She looked at him across the room, started to speak, and then smiled faintly and walked down the hall.

"Dani..."

She didn't turn. "Yes?"

There was a long, trembling silence. "My room is the first door to the left," he said thickly. "The bed...is large enough for all three of us."

Tears stung her eyes. "If you don't mind," she whispered.

"Mind!" He was behind her, beside her; he had her in his arms, close and warm and protected. His mouth found hers in a single graceful motion. She clung. He lifted her, devoured her. His dark eyes sought hers as he kissed her.

"Now?" he whispered, trembling.

"Now," she moaned huskily.

He bent to her mouth again and she trembled with delicious anticipation as he carried her slowly into his bedroom and closed the door behind them.

Two weeks later she had to go back home for her checkup, and to hire someone else to help Harriett at the bookstore. Dutch flew back with her since the weekend was coming up. But he had to be in Chicago for a conference on Monday.

"I don't like leaving you here," he said curtly, glaring around at her small apartment. She'd become so much a part of his life that it felt odd to leave her behind.

She didn't want the parting, either, but she hadn't switched to a Chicago doctor yet, and she needed to be sure about the baby.

"Don't worry about me," she told him, holding his big hand in hers as she walked him to the door. "I'll be fine. The nights will last forever, but I'll manage," she teased.

He didn't smile. He touched her cheek, feeling tremors all the way to his soul. It was because of the baby that he felt this uneasy, he told himself. Only because of the baby. "I'll be back day after tomorrow," he said. "We'll spend the week here, getting things in order. Tell Harriett I said to look after you."

"Harrie will." She smiled. "Do I get a good-bye kiss?"

He pulled her against his tall frame. "I wonder if I'll make it out the door if I kiss you?" he murmured with a dry smile. "Come here."

He drew her up on her tiptoes and covered her smiling mouth with his. It was like flying, he mused, eyes closing as he savored the taste of her. Flying, floating. She made his head light. He lifted his lips finally and searched her loving eyes. It didn't bother him so much these days, that adoration. Perhaps he'd gotten used to it.

He brushed a last kiss against her lips. "Behave. And watch these steps, okay?"

"Okay. 'Bye."

He touched her hair. " 'Bye." He walked away without looking back. She closed the door, and realized she hadn't felt so alone since her parents had walked away from her years and years ago.

Ten

Harriett was all ears, fascinated by the news that Dani's unlikely husband was actually going to try to settle down.

"He must feel something for you," she said, smiling at Dani. "I don't care what you say, no man is going to go to those lengths just because of a purely physical involvement."

Dani had been afraid to think that, much less say it. But she stared at Harriett for a long time, wondering.

"In some ways you're still very naive, my friend," Harriett said with a wicked grin. "He's hooked. He just hasn't realized it yet."

If only it were true, Dani thought, praying for a miracle. If only he liked the job Apollo offered him. Even moving to Chicago wouldn't be any hardship. Harriett and Dave would visit. And she could come back to Greenville from time to time. Harriett could be godmother. She smiled.

With her mind on Dutch, not on what she was doing, she went to step up on the long ladder against the wall to get a book from a high shelf. She was halfway up when she slipped. Terrified, screaming as she hit the floor, she looked up at Harriett, her face white.

"Oh, God, the baby!" she sobbed, clutching her stomach.

"It's all right," Harriett said quickly, soothing her. "It's all right, I'll get an ambulance. Lie still! Are you hurt anywhere?"

"I don't know!"

Harriett ran for the phone. Dani lay there, panic-stricken, clutching her stomach. No, please don't let me lose my baby, she prayed. Her eyes closed and tears bled from them as the first pain began to make itself felt in her leg, in her back. Please, please, please!

The next few minutes were a nightmare of waiting, worrying. The ambulance came, the attendants got her on the stretcher, took her to the hospital, and into the emergency room, with Harriett right behind. She hardly knew Harriett was there, she was so afraid of losing the baby.

She was examined by the emergency room doctor, who would tell her nothing. Then the tests began and went on and on until finally they took her to a room and left her, shaking with worry. Her doctor would talk to her when they got the test results, she was informed.

She cried and cried. Harriett tried to soothe her, but it was useless. She was feeling a dragging pain in lower stomach, and she knew she was going to lose the baby. She was going to lose her baby! Harriett asked her for something, a name in Chicago to call, to tell Dutch. Numbly, she gave her J.D. Brettman's name and closed her eyes. It was no use, she wanted to say. Dutch would come, but only out of responsibility...and then she remembered the other time, the other pregnant woman, and she was terrified of what he might do.

Dr. Carter came walking in a few hours later, took one look at her and went back out to call for a sedative. He came in again, took her hand and nodded Harriett toward the door. He didn't speak until she was gone.

"The baby's going to be fine," he said. "So are you. Now, calm down."

The tears stopped, although her eyes remained wet and red. "What?"

"The baby's all right." He smiled, his blue eyes twinkling. "Babies are tough. They've got all that fluid around them, wonderful protection. Of course, you're bruised a little here and there, but bruises heal. You'll be fine."

She leaned back with a sigh. "Thank God," she said. "Oh, thank God. But—but these dragging pains," she added, pressing her stomach.

"False labor. A few twinges are normal," he said, grinning. "Now, stop worrying, will you?"

The nurse came in with a syringe, but before she could go any farther, the door flew open and a blond man burst into the room with eyes so wild that both doctor and nurse actually backed up a step.

"Eric!" Dani whispered, astonished at the look on his face.

He went to her, a wet, disheveled raincoat over his gray suit. He was wild-eyed, flushed as if he'd been running, and half out of breath.

"You're all right?" he asked unsteadily, touching her as if he expected to find broken limbs. "The baby's all right?"

"Yes," she whispered. "Eric, it's all right!" she repeated softly, and the look on his face was the answer to a prayer. "It's all right, I just fell off the ladder, but I'm—"

"Oh, God." He sat down beside her. The hands that touched her trembled, and there was a look in his eyes that struck her dumb. He caressed her face and suddenly bent, burying his face in her throat. "Oh, God." He was shaking!

Her arms went up and around him, hesitantly, her hands smoothing his hair, comforting him. She felt something wet against her throat and felt her own eyes being to sting.

"Oh, darling," she whispered, holding him closer. Her eyes closed as the enormity of what he felt for her was laid bare, without a word being spoken. She laughed through her tears. She could conquer the world now. She could do anything! He loved her!

"Reaction," the doctor said, nodding. He took the syringe from the nurse. "Pregnancy is hard on fathers, too," he murmured dryly. "Off with that coat, young man." He removed the raincoat, and the suitcoat, then rolled up the sleeve of the shirt without any help from Dutch, who wouldn't let go of Dani, and jabbed the needle into the muscular arm. "I'll have a daybed rolled in here, because you aren't driving anywhere. Dani, I think you'd do without a sedative now, am I right?" he added with a grin.

"Yes, sir," she whispered, smiling dreamily as she rocked her husband in her arms.

He nodded and went out with the nurse, closing the door behind him.

"I love you," Dani whispered adoringly. "I love you, I love you, I love you...."

His mouth stopped the words, tenderly seeking, probing, and his lips trembled against hers.

He lifted his head to look at her, unashamedly letting her see the traces of wetness on his cheeks. "J.D. came himself to tell me after Harriett called." He touched her face hesitantly. "I went crazy," he confessed absently. "J.D. got me a seat on the next plane. I ran out of the terminal and took a cab away from some people.... I don't even remember how I got here." He bent and brushed his mouth softly against hers as he let the relief wash over him. His wife. His heart. "I was...I was going to call you tonight. I wanted to tell you how much I like what I'll be doing. I found us a house," he added slowly. "On the beach, with a fenced yard. It will be nice, for the baby."

"Yes, darling," she whispered softly.

He brushed the hair back from her face. "I was so afraid of what I'd find in here," he said unsteadily. "All I could think was that I'd only just realized what I felt for you, and so quickly it could have ended. I would have been alone again."

"As long as I'm alive, you'll never be alone," she whispered.

He touched her mouth, her throat, her swollen stomach. "Danielle, I love you," he whispered breathlessly, admitting it at last, awe in his whole look.

"Yes, I know," she answered on a jubilant little laugh.

He laughed, too. "I've never said that before. It isn't hard." He looked into her eyes. "I love you."

She smiled, stretching. "I love you, too. Ooh," she groaned, touching her back. "I'm bruised all over. That stupid ladder!"

"No more stupid ladders," he said firmly. "We're moving to Chicago, where I can watch you. Harriett can visit."

Her eyes searched his. "This is what you really want?"

"How can I take care of you from across the world?" he asked reasonably. His voice was slowing, and he looked drowsy. "Anyway, I was getting too old for it. And I like the challenge of teaching techniques I've learned." He kissed her softly again. "J.D. told me I could do it. When he and Gabby got married, he decided that marriage was more exciting than dodging bullets. I think he has something there."

He looked down at her stomach and the last of the barriers came down. "He's going to be all right, they're sure?" he asked touching the swell.

Her lips parted, smiling. She sat up and touched his face with soft, loving hands. "I'm giving you a baby," she whispered, smiling. "A healthy, strong boy. The doctor said so."

He started to speak, and couldn't. And tried again. "I'll take care of you both," he whispered.

She reached forward and caught his full lower lip gently between her teeth. "I'll take care of you, just as soon as they let me out of here," she teased.

He chuckled softly, putting a hand to his temple. "I may need taking care of. My God, what was in that syringe?"

"A sedative. They brought it for me, but I guess they decided you needed it more."

He smiled ruefully. "I'd like to talk some more, but I think I'd feel better lying down."

Dr. Carter came in with a nurse and a spare bed even as the words were echoing in the room. He glanced at his watch and grinned at Dutch. "I thought you'd be about ready for this. Lie down, father-to-be, and you can both have a nice nap until supper. Feeling okay now, Dani?'' he asked.

"Just wonderful." She sighed, trading soft looks with her drowsy husband. The nurse was eyeing him wistfully, and Dani only smiled with confidence of a woman who is deeply loved. As Dutch lay down her eyes closed on the smile he gave her. Minutes later she was asleep, with the future lying open and bright ahead.

Eleven

The christening took place six months later, with little two-month-old Joshua van Meer cradled in his mother's arms. At Dani's side Dutch burned with pride in his young son, and amused looks passed among an odd group on the front pew of the Presbyterian church in the outskirts of Chicago.

Harriett felt uneasy, sitting next to them all, and Dave had actually started to get up except that she'd caught him in time. What a collection of unusual men, she thought, gaping. There was an older, wiry little man sitting beside a wiry, tough-looking woman and they were holding hands. There were two black men, a tall, dignified one and a shorter, grinning one. There was a huge dark-eyed, dark-headed man sitting beside a green-eyed brunette who was obviously pregnant. On the other side was a swarthy Latin, arms folded, looking elegant. Harriett turned her attention back to the minister, who had taken the child in his arms and was walking it up and down the rows of pews. Harriett smiled. Her godchild. Dani had wanted her to stand with them during the ceremony, but she'd twisted her ankle getting on the airplane, and could hardly manage to stand. Just as well, she thought with a smile at the big blond Dutchman. She and that handsome giant were too much alike to ever get along. But even she had to admit that he was a terrific husband and father. A surprisingly domestic man, all around. A really normal man. Except for his friends here.

After the ceremony was over, the group beside Harriett sat still. She wondered for a wild minute if they were escaped fugitives, because they seemed to be looking around them all the time.

Dani rushed forward and hugged her. "Wasn't Joshua good?" she asked enthusiastically, kissing the white-clad baby in her arms. He cooed up at her. "I was so proud of him! Harrie, you haven't met our friends. Gabby!"

Gabby Darwin Brettman drew her tall husband along with her, beaming as she made faces at the baby.

"Isn't he gorgeous! I want a girl myself," Gabby said, her bright green eyes gleaming, "but J.D.'s holding out for a boy."

"I don't care what it is, as long as it's ours," J.D. grinned. "Hi, Dani. Nice ceremony. Dutch didn't even pass out; I was proud of him."

"Imagine Dutch married." The wiry old man shook his head. "And with a child!"

"Could have knocked me over with a feather when I found out," the tall black man joined in.

"Hush, First Shirt," Gabby growled at the older man. "And shame on you, Apollo," she told the tall black man. "Dutch just had to find the right girl, that's all."

Apollo shrugged. "Well, I'm glad he did," he told Dani with twinkling eyes, "because he's sure made the best vice-president any consulting firm could ask for. Shirt, when are you going to give in and join up? Semson and Drago already did. And I need someone to teach defensive driving."

"You corporate tycoons give me a pain," First Shirt scoffed. "Besides, Mrs. Darwin and I are contemplating a merger." He grinned at the blushing widow beside him, who was Gabby's mother, from Lytle, Texas. "We're going to raise cattle and sand."

"I owe it all to J.D.," Apollo said, smiling warmly at the big, dark man beside Gabby. "He got me off. Years of hiding, over. I'm glad you decided to go into law, J.D."

"So am I," J.D. replied. He looked up as Dutch joined them. "I was just coming to find you. Gabby and I are starting natural childbirth classes. Any advice?"

Dutch grinned as he put an affectionate arm around Dani. "Sure. Go buy a can of tennis balls."

Gabby stared at him. "Tennis...balls?"

"Tennis balls." He leaned forward conspiratorially. "They're for your backache. J.D. is supposed to roll them up and down your spine."

"It really does help," Dani said. She bent and kissed her son. "The best part is when you get to hold him for the first time."

"Yes," Dutch agreed. "Let's go grill some steaks," he said. "Everybody know how to get to our place?"

"Sure," Apollo said. "I'll lead the ones who don't. You got enough steaks?"

"Shirt and Mrs. Darwin brought a boxful. If we make you stand last in line, there should be enough to go around," he said with a grin.

Apollo glared at him. "I don't eat that much!"

"Only half a ham at a time," Dutch shot back. "Remember Angola, when you ate the rabbit I'd just snared?"

"Oh, yeah, remember 'Nam, when you ate the snake I caught?"

"It's a christening," J.D. said, separating them. "We're supposed to forget old grudges at a time like this."

They both turned at him. "Yeah?" Apollo asked. "Well, you're the turkey that ate the box of cookies my mother sent me...."

"And the plum pudding I scrounged from the camp cook," Dutch added in the same breath.

J.D. drew Gabby beside him. "You can't pick on a man with a pregnant wife."

"I had one of my own until two months ago," Dutch returned.

"Well, I'm not standing too close to you guys," Apollo said gruffly, eyeing them. "It might be contagious."

"You won't get pregnant, Apollo, honest," Dutch said with a wicked grin.

Apollo glared at him and moved away. "Funny man. You know I meant this marriage virus."

"Some virus." J.D. grinned, hugging Gabby close. "What a way to go!"

Dani was laughing wildly, along with Gabby and the others. She moved close to Dutch and nuzzled her dark head against his shoulder. "I'm starved. Let's go home. We've got all kinds of stuff to eat."

"Yes, well, let's just make sure Apollo doesn't get there before us," J.D. teased.

Apollo glared at him. "I'm returning the Christmas present I bought you."

"It's almost March," J.D. reminded him.

"That gives you ten months to look forward to not getting one," Apollo said smugly.

"Come on," Dutch chuckled. "Let's go celebrate."

"Yes," Dani said, so that only Dutch could hear. "I have a different kind of celebration in mind for later," she murmured. "My doctor said I could."

Dutch's eyes lit up as he studied her bright eyes. "Did he? Hmmm," he murmured, drawing her close to his side and smiling down at the baby sleeping in her arms. "Well, we'll have to think up some new things to try, won't we?" he asked, watching her with smug delight. He whispered into her ear, and despite months of marriage and a baby, she colored delightfully.

She felt more alive than she ever had in her life. She looked up at him with such love that the roomful of people seemed to disappear. His fingers touched her mouth.

"Tonight," he whispered, holding her gaze, "I'll love you the way I loved you that morning in Veracruz."

"You'll get me pregnant again," she whispered, her heart throbbing wildly.

His own breath caught. "We'll talk about it tonight."

"Yes." She searched his eyes slowly. "No regrets?"

He shook his head. "Not one. Watching that

She reached up and touched his hard cheek gently. He smiled, and for a moment, they were alone in the world.

READERS' COMMENTS ON SILHOUETTE DESIRES

"Thank you for Silhouette Desires. They are the best thing that has happened to the bookshelves in a long time."

—V.W.*, Knoxville, TN

"Silhouette Desires—wonderful, fantastic—the best romance around."

—H.T.*, Margate, N.J.

"As a writer as well as a reader of romantic fiction, I found DESIREs most refreshingly realistic—and definitely as magical as the love captured on their pages."

—C.M.*, Silver Lake, N.Y.

"I just wanted to let you know how very much I enjoy your Silhouette Desire books. I read other romances, and I must say your books rate up at the top of the list."

—C.N.*, Anaheim, CA

"Desires are number one. I especially enjoy the endings because they just don't leave you with a kiss or embrace; they finish the story. Thank you for giving me such reading pleasure."

—M.S.*, Sandford, FL

*names available on request

READERS' COMMENTS ON SILHOUETTE SPECIAL EDITIONS:

"I just finished reading the first six Silhouette Special Edition Books and I had to take the opportunity to write you and tell you how much I enjoyed them. I enjoyed all the authors in this series. Best wishes on your Silhouette Special Editions line and many thanks."

—B.H.*, Jackson, OH

"The Special Editions are really special and I enjoyed them very much! I am looking forward to next month's books."

—R.M.W.*, Melbourne, FL

"I've just finished reading four of your first six Special Editions and I enjoyed them very much. I like the more sensual detail and longer stories. I will look forward each month to your new Special Editions."

—L.S.*, Visalia, CA

"Silhouette Special Editions are — 1.) Superb! 2.) Great! 3.) Delicious! 4.) Fantastic! . . . Did I leave anything out? These are books that an adult woman can read . . . I love them!"

—H.C.*, Monterey Park, CA

*names available on request

Silhouette Desire
COMING NEXT MONTH

GOLDEN GODDESS—Stephanie James
With the appearance of a golden fertility goddess in her luggage and a handsome stranger in her hotel room, Hannah Prescott's Hawaiian vacation was proving to be anything but restful!

RIVER OF DREAMS—Naomi Horton
Traveling up the Amazon was a dangerous proposition, but Leigh didn't realize that the greatest danger lay in the arms of the emerald-eyed riverman she'd hired to guide her.

TO HAVE IT ALL—Robin Elliott
Brant Adams wanted a wife and family. He wanted Jenna Winters, but Brant didn't understand that love means trusting and sharing, and she would accept no less.

LEADER OF THE PACK—Diana Stuart
While dogsled racing across the Alaskan wilderness, Weylin Matthews and Jenna Hendersen were locked in a heated battle—until an accident cooled their anger and ignited the fires of desire.

FALSE IMPRESSIONS—Ariel Berk
Anthropologist Audrey Lampert was posing as a waitress at the Angel Club to study the male clientele, but Brandon Fox had less studious pursuits in mind.

WINTER MEETING—Doreen Owens Malek
Kyle Reardon had been proved guilty, yet Leda desperately hoped that the verdict was wrong. How could she be in love with the man responsible for her father's death?

AVAILABLE NOW:

BEYOND LOVE
Ann Major

THE TENDER STRANGER
Diana Palmer

MOON MADNESS
Freda Vasilos

STARLIGHT
Penelope Wisdom

YEAR OF THE POET
Ann Hurley

A BIRD IN HAND
Dixie Browning